Diapers, Drama, and Deceit

The Mothers of Easthaven

by

Erina Bridget Ring

Cover design by Rae Monet, Inc. (www.raemonetinc.com)
Edited by Carolyn Woolston
Formatted by Self-Publishing Services LLC (www.Self-Publishing-Service.com)

A mother's love is never-ending

Acknowledgments

My heartfelt thanks to my husband, Jack, and my children for their constant support. It is on our walk through life that we find friends who give support as well, and I would also like to thank Kay O'Bryon, Beverly Smith-Mediavilla, and Gene Tartaglia. Finally, without the support of my editor and good friend Carolyn Woolston, I would never have written a single word.

Erina Bridget Ring
Napa, California, 2015

Prologue

Dear Janel,

Remember our baby group? Remember how the group came together, and how we were all excited about having playmates for the girls? Looking back on it, I have to ask myself why I didn't see what was coming. How could we have been so innocent?

I ran into Samantha today at the grocery store. Remember her? I have not seen her or talked to her for decades…she told me news about some of the women from the group. I thought you would be interested.

Love to your family,

Ava

Oak Tree Park

The park down the street from my house had a winding path that led to a beautiful oak tree. The trunk was gnarly and the branches reached majestically over the playground, shading the entire area. A cluster of benches lined the path, and parents sat there and watched their children play. Lavender violas and pink asters grew along the edge of the path, with bluebonnets and a sprinkle of yellow and white daisies. Lush green grass spread as far as you could see.

There were two play areas, one with a sandbox, short slide, and swings for toddlers, and a larger one on the other side of the path for older kids. I thought it was the perfect place for moms to gather.

I was an avid walker and since the birth of my daughter, Jill, a month ago, I was taking long daily rambles. I would get up early and take my older children, Gina and Jay, to school and then I walked to the park with Jill. There was something special about this park; no matter how sleep-deprived I was, the beautiful scenery lifted my spirits. Life was full and good.

I first met Janel on a Wednesday morning when we were both walking along the twisting path with our babies in their strollers and we came to a curve where the strollers could not pass. We stopped, and instead of walking on past each other, we began to chat.

"Hello there," I said. I peeked into her stroller and saw an adorable baby with a little white hat covering her head and a pair of beautiful big brown eyes looking up at me. "I see you have a little girl."

The woman laughed. She had a pink stroller with a pink blanket draped on it, and her daughter was dressed in a darling pink and white outfit.

"I'm Ava," I said. "And this is my daughter, Jill."

"My name is Janel, and my baby's name is Mandy."

Janel was in her earlier thirties, a petite Asian woman a little over five feet tall with shoulder-length straight black hair and a glowing skin that needed no makeup. She wore jeans, a loose red tee-shirt with a Nike logo, and denim slip-on flats. She was soft-spoken, and I could see her cultural traditions peek through as she bowed her head ever so slightly when she extended her hand to shake mine.

"How old is your daughter?" she asked.

"One month, born in May."

"So is my daughter!"

"How is she sleeping?" I ventured.

"Not well. She wakes up every two or three hours."

I laughed. "Same here."

Janel and I bonded immediately. By the time we walked all the way to the bench under the oak tree we had discovered that we were both stay-at-home moms, we each had older children, and our husbands traveled a lot. Soon we were talking about babies, sleepless nights, and early wakeup calls to take our older children to school.

Janel offered me a cup of hot chocolate from her thermos and we sat under the tree talking about pacifiers, new kinds of baby bottles, even the geometry and history classes our older kids were taking. We both admitted we let our infants sleep in our bedrooms, a cardinal No-No for new parents trying to train their babies to sleep by themselves. We didn't care what the rules were; we did what felt good to us.

Janel and I had a lot in common, and time just flew by. It turned out that Janel's husband, Rich, was vice president of a major telecommunications company and traveled overseas, as my husband, James, did. We talked about how hard it was when they were gone. That first day we talked for two hours, exchanged phone numbers, and decided to meet at the park the following week. When we got to the edge of the winding path we hugged each other like old friends.

It was then that the idea of forming a baby play group began to percolate.

* * *

The weekend passed quickly, and Sunday morning my whole family attended St. Anthony's church just a few miles from home. We knew almost everyone in the warm, welcoming community, and today we sat toward the back in case Jill cried. Right behind us I noticed a handsome couple holding a cute baby dressed in pink with a matching bonnet. I couldn't tell how old she was, but as we were leaving, the woman whispered, "I want to talk to you after church."

She was tall and trim, wearing black slacks. Her husband was also tall and wore khaki slacks and a white shirt. They both smiled at James and me, and she touched little Jill's foot.

"I'm Taylor Carter, and this is my husband, Brandon. All through Mass I noticed your daughter. Our daughter, Megan, is six weeks old." I smiled at her and introduced James.

Taylor looked to be in her early thirties, a beautiful woman wearing very little makeup and just a hint of lip gloss. Her curly black hair was cut to hug the nape of her neck.

"Brandon and I moved to Easthaven just last week, from New Jersey."

I looked at her in surprise. "Wow, a move with a newborn baby!"

"Yes. I still wake up surprised."

Brandon just smiled. "I got a job promotion," he said. Taylor rolled her eyes. Apparently moving was a sore spot for the two of them. I sensed that Taylor was tired, which was understandable, but

9

something else nagged at me, and in an instant I knew what I was going to do.

"Taylor, I'm meeting a friend and her new baby on Wednesday at Oak Tree Park. Would you like to join us?"

Her face lit up and she grinned. "Oh, Ava, I would love to! Can I bring something?"

"Oh, no. I'm bringing coffee. Just bring Megan." I dug in my wallet for a bank deposit slip to write my name and phone number; Taylor gave me her business card. We said goodbye until Wednesday.

Later that day I took Jill to the supermarket to pick up something for dinner; I was in the produce department when I heard someone say my name. I look up from a nicely stacked tower of apples and there was Sonja Travers.

"Sonja, how are you?" I was running late but I tried not to sound hurried.

"Ava, I'm exhausted. Kenny has his nights and days mixed up." I could hear the exhaustion in her voice and I just listened while trying to count out six apples and secure the tie around the plastic bag.

I had known Sonja for years. We first met at a coffee shop downtown that she and her husband frequented. She was 39, a chunky five foot seven, and she looked older than her age. Her skin was wrinkled from years of playing tennis in the sun and her hair was frizzy and sun-bleached. Today she was wearing shorts and a matching shirt that had baby spit-up all over it. Her hair was uncombed, the dark roots showing, and she wore only one earring. Sonja always wore coordinated clothes, and she loved costume jewelry. She also loved throwing parties and decorating her home for each holiday. She was always the life of the party.

Sonja's husband, Mitch, was a physician in Easthaven, and people loved him. He was quiet; she was extroverted. When we first met, my son Jay was two years old and Gina was in pre-school. I told Sonja and Mitch that we had just joined the Easthaven country club and we played a lot of tennis.

Kenny was crying his lungs out in the grocery cart seat. Sonja sighed. "I had no idea it would be so tough having an infant!" She looked haggard.

"It's rough the first few years," I said.

"Years!" she blurted. "Oh, my God. You make it look so easy, Ava."

I blinked at that. "Whatever gave you that impression? I don't think I ever said raising children was easy for anyone."

Sonja and I were still standing in the middle of the produce department when a woman with an infant in her arms jostled past me to reach the apples. She looked harried, and suddenly she looked up.

"I'm Merrick Shoemaker." Sonja and I introduced ourselves and we began to talk right there in the produce aisle. The longer we stood there the more Merrick told us about what a rough time she was having. Finally she asked if we knew of any groups for mothers and infants. "My father is dying, my husband travels, and I'm taking care of a baby. I'm starved for adult conversation."

"Come to the park next Wednesday," I invited. "A few women with infants are meeting there for the first time." I looked at Sonja. "You're invited, too."

Merrick was in her mid-thirties with beautiful blonde hair down to her waist. She was tall and thin and extremely pretty, with a small voice that was a bit raspy. She wore tan slacks with a frilly long-sleeved white blouse, tan shoes, and a tan belt. She also wore the biggest diamond earrings I had ever seen, and from the size of her diamond wedding ring I knew she was well-off.

Merrick and Sonja and I parted, and just as I turned to go into the meat department, there was Ruthanne, wearing jeans and a stained shirt. She was holding her new baby and looking dazed. Ruthanne rarely left her house without makeup and she always wore the latest fashions from New York; but today there was something different about her. Her clothes looked disheveled and her face was sad.

"Ava!" she said loudly. She patted Jill's head. "Don't look at me. I've been up with Jon every night this week, all night. It's been brutal."

She looked so frazzled I invited her to the Wednesday meeting at the park. When I got home an hour and a half later, James wanted to know what had taken me so long.

"I'm organizing a baby group and I ran into everyone at the store."

"That's great, Ava. You loved your baby group when our older kids were little."

I had always been a stay-at-home mom. I was 33, a petite 5 foot 1, with a 12-year-old daughter and a 10-year-old son. And now our one-month-old daughter, Jill. Usually I wore jeans and black tee-shirts or black sweaters and flat shoes for comfort, and I always carried a clean tee-shirt in case Jill spit up all over me.

James was in engineering, and he owned his own business and traveled extensively. We entertained often, usually on very short notice, and many times I found I was the youngest wife in the group. Sometimes I sensed the other women were critical of me.

James and I often joked that we were a tag team when the kids had to be in two different places at the same time. Having older children at school all day gave me plenty of one-on-one time with Jill. When Gina and Jay were young, I had organized a baby group for companionship, not only for the kids but for myself, too. That group was instrumental in finding out the latest about child care, and the mothers often had serious discussions about politics and even religious beliefs. For me it was mostly to enjoy the friendship of other women going through the same struggles I was. It was comforting to have a shoulder to cry on if something terrible was happening to one of us, and it was wonderful to have a friend to call if I was having a bad day.

When Jill was born I knew it was just a matter of time before I would start another baby group. I just didn't realize it would come together so quickly.

The Gathering

Wednesday morning came and Jill had not slept much the night before. Around 6 a.m. I finally stopped trying to get her to sleep and climbed out of bed. In my mirror I saw noticeable bags under my eyes. Makeup would only accentuate them, so I left them alone and just combed my hair. A shower would have to wait until Jill took her morning nap.

I yawned and started to brew my coffee. Today I was hosting the baby group for the first time, so I arrived at the park early with two large thermoses of coffee and a Tupperware bowl of fresh fruit and slices of bundt cake. I was just placing my wedding band quilt on the grass for the babies and moms to sit on when I noticed Janel coming up the path. I smiled and leaned in to hug her and give Mandy a kiss on her forehead.

"I invited a few other women to join us today. I hope that's okay with you?"

"Oh, Ava, that sounds wonderful."

We sat the babies on my quilt and then Taylor Carter arrived. She was not in a good mood.

"Boy, what a morning I've had!" she complained loudly. "Brandon left for Tokyo three days ago and I'm exhausted. Megan's not sleeping and Brandon just called to inform me his trip has been extended another week."

Janel and I just waited, then Taylor moved Megan to the quilt on the grass and I patted the baby's head. Taylor looked sad. When she stood up I gave her a hug. "Call me anytime you need a little break," I said. "I could watch Megan and you could take a nap. Any time this week."

She looked at me in surprise and burst into tears. Janel and I just stood there. Still teary-eyed, Taylor then said, "That's the nicest thing anyone has ever offered me."

"I'm just a phone call away," I told her.

Taylor wiped her eyes, and I had just finished introducing her to Janel when Janel started to laugh. "What's so funny?" Taylor asked with a frown.

"Look at Megan and Mandy and Jill," Janel said. "Our kids look like munchkins compared to Megan!"

Laughing, I took my camera out and snapped a photo.

Merrick Shoemaker arrived next, pushing her stroller as determinedly as if she were on a mission, a little hunched over and almost running behind it. "I am so tired I almost didn't come," she said, out of breath.

I wondered if she would cry as Taylor Carter had. Merrick's son, Bobby, was sound asleep in his stroller.

"Wouldn't it be nice," I said, "if *we* had strollers to crawl into and nap like that?"

"I would just like to nap whenever I wanted to," Janel added. We chuckled, and then Sonja and Kenny arrived.

"Hello, everyone!" Sonja said loudly. She startled Bobby, who began to cry.

Merrick glared at her. "Now look what you've done!" Sonja apologized, but Merrick was having none of it.

Whew. I needed to diffuse this situation, so I started to pour the coffee.

"Is this everyone?" Janel asked. At that moment Ruthanne walked up the path toward us, wearing a very short mini-skirt, a blouse with a very low V-neck, and 4-inch heels. She was pushing Jon in his stroller.

I had never seen Ruthanne in full face makeup before, but I hid my surprise and we all sat down, watching her carefully maneuver her way onto the quilt. Her skirt rode up and she finally had to take off her heels to get down onto the quilt without tipping over. "It's a good thing I have my blouse taped," she announced.

I had no idea what she meant until one side of her blouse came loose and one breast hung out. Ruthanne let out a yelp. "Oops, sorry."

No one said a word. Not one word. Her son Jon started to cry, and Ruthanne started to nurse him right there. She had no blanket to cover up with and no burp cloth; she just moved her blouse aside. I saw Janel look up at the sky.

Sonja wanted to know more about the tape Ruthanne was using for her blouse. Merrick Shoemaker and Taylor Carter couldn't stop staring, and I could see they were uncomfortable with the situation, so I handed Ruthanne a little lightweight blanket to cover herself up with.

"This quilt is beautiful," she said.

"It was a gift to James and me on our wedding day. It belonged to James's mother's great-great aunt Nelly, who died when she was a hundred and three." The quilt was large enough for a king-sized bed and had wedding ring patterns adorning it, each ring with multiple colors and shapes within it, joined together at the center; they looked like half-circles if you looked closely. No two rings were exactly the same, and the pattern was soft pastel blues and light green with touches of yellow and rose; the background was white with a rose border.

"You could sell this for a lot of money," Ruthanne said. "Quilts are in."

What an odd thing to say! "This is a family heirloom," I said quickly. "One that I treasure. I would never sell it."

The other women admired it, and then Janel defused the situation. "It's a wonderful day to be sitting on this quilt in the shade under this beautiful oak tree with all of you."

Conversation resumed and I overheard Ruthanne ask Sonja, "When was the last time you and your husband had sex?" Everyone went quiet at such a personal question. Ruthanne looked at us and said proudly, "Walter and I are back at it."

Sonja said, "If Mitch so much as comes near me, I'll shoot him. I'm just too tired these days."

Merrick said those were her sentiments exactly. "Could you imagine having another baby nine months from now? I want one more," she added, "but not now.

Janel and I looked at each other and kept quiet.

"What happened with you, Ava?" Ruthanne asked.

"What do you mean?"

"Your older kids are close in age, and then ten years later you have Jill."

I cleared my throat. How much information is too much, I thought. "We were lucky to have Jill. She is a gift."

"Oh, my God, Ruthanne," Merrick said in her low, somewhat raspy voice. "You can see Ava isn't comfortable with this conversation. Leave her alone." Janel agreed, and Ruthanne began to sulk.

To change the conversation I offered some fresh fruit to the women. Maybe when we got to know each other better I would open up on this subject. Then the chatter turned to our children. Everyone wanted to know how we had all come together today. We were all enjoying our coffee when someone spilled a bit on the quilt. "Please don't worry about it," I said quickly. "I can get the stain out."

"Does anyone have older children?" Janel asked. "I have an eight-year-old son, Tim."

"What does your husband do?" Ruthanne blurted.

"He works in communications," Janel said, her voice quiet.

"What exactly does that mean?"

"That means he works in telecommunications," Janel said tactfully.

"Whoa," Ruthanne exclaimed. "He must make a lot of money."

All of us stared at her. No one asks that kind of question, at least not with other people present. What Janel had omitted to say was that her husband was vice president of his telecommunications firm.

The women ignored the exchange, and then Taylor said, "My husband is in sales. He travels all over the place."

"Do you travel with him?" Ruthanne asked.

"No, I don't get the chance now, with the baby."

Merrick Shoemaker said her husband worked for the utility company and traveled state-wide. Sonja sat playing with the babies and finally spoke. "Mitch, my husband, is a physician here in Easthaven."

Ruthanne opened her mouth, but I jumped in. "James is starting up his own business, and I stay at home with our three children."

Taylor Carter wanted to know why I didn't work.

"But I do work," I said. "I'm working harder than I ever have before."

I must have sounded terse because Merrick Shoemaker said, "It's a noble thing to stay at home and raise your own children. I love it. Robert, my husband, wouldn't have it any other way."

"So you don't work, either?" Taylor Carter remarked. Merrick did not reply.

Sonja looked over at Ruthanne. "What do you do, Ruthanne?"

"My husband," Ruthanne answered slowly, "is climbing the corporate ladder in sales. He travels internationally, and I travel with him every chance I get." She paused. "I am sure all your husbands make six figures."

One of the women gasped. "Do you work, Ruthanne?" Sonja asked.

"Yes. I am a physician's assistant. I do everything a doctor does."

Sonja perked up at that. "Where did you go to school?"

"Valley College."

"But that's a community college. Don't you need a four-year college degree to be a physician's assistant? It's almost like going to medical school."

Ruthanne was silent.

"Anyone want coffee?" I interrupted.

Ruthanne looked uncomfortable and said nothing, but Sonja didn't let the subject drop and things started to get tense. Ruthanne finally picked up her son and acted as if she hadn't heard the remark about medical school.

From then on I had a funny feeling that there was something Ruthanne was not telling us. I couldn't put my finger on it; I just had an odd feeling about her.

The conversation went on about babies and everyone seemed to be having a good time, and the next thing I heard was Merrick Shoemaker inviting us all over to her house next Wednesday morning. Everyone scrambled for pen and paper to write down phone numbers and suddenly Taylor pulled out business cards for each of the women. They glanced at the card and then at Taylor. "Wow," Sonja said. "How professional of you! What a great idea."

I returned home shortly after noon, changed Jill's diaper, and filled another bottle and put it in the diaper bag I kept ready by the front door. Gina and Jay scrambled into the car and I drove to their friend Gary's house. I asked Gary's mother, Marilyn, how she was doing.

"Summer is driving me crazy," she said. "The kids want to be anywhere but home, and I'm exhausted from their bickering." I half-smiled and said I understood.

"It's going to be a long summer," she said. "My husband has taken a new job out of state. It's a great opportunity for him."

"Do you have family where you'll be moving?"

"They all live here," she said. "And now I'm moving away."

"On the other hand," I said, "maybe it will take you and your kids on a new adventure, and maybe later you'll end up back here!"

Marilyn started to cry. With Jill in one arm I put my other arm around her. When she offered me some iced tea, I couldn't refuse.

Our visit ended four hours later, and when we got back to the house, James was home from work, Jill needed to be fed, and I needed to get dinner on.

"How was your day, honey?" my husband asked after a long day of work. I threw my arms around him and gave him a big kiss and an extra-long hug.

"What was that for?"

"We are so lucky to live here. The kids are all doing well. Life is good. Do I need a better reason?" I delved into the fridge to get chicken and vegetables for dinner.

"We had our first baby group meeting in the park today. It's an interesting group of women. One of them turned up in a mini-skirt and high heels and wanted to know how much money everyone's husband made. It was embarrassing."

James raised his eyebrows. "Someone wore a mini-skirt?" He chuckled.

"The same woman tried to get us to talk about our sex lives," I went on. "That was a tad uncomfortable."

His eyebrows went up again. "Is that what you women talk about at these baby groups?" he said with a smile.

"Another mother, Taylor Carter, said she'd had such a bad morning she cried, but once we started talking about our children and how we were coping she said she didn't feel so alone."

"Looks like I'll have to be in Korea in two weeks," he said. "And the trip might last at least several weeks."

"Oh, no," I sighed. "I have a newborn and Gina and Jay have busy schedules. I depend on your help."

"We'll make it work, honey." But I knew *I* was the one who had to make it work. James had no choice when it came to long trips overseas, but I understood that he dreaded them as much as I did. I continued cooking dinner and thought about how interesting the baby group was turning out to be.

"Ring the Doorbell"

Wednesday morning came, and after I dropped the older kids off I drove to Merrick's house, surprised that she lived just a few blocks away. I thought it was odd that I'd never seen her in the neighborhood before.

I knocked on her door and stood waiting with Jill in my arms. No answer. A few minutes passed, and then Taylor arrived with Megan.

She smoothed her short black curls. "Have you knocked on the door already?"

"Yes, about five minutes ago." While we waited we chatted about our babies being up in the middle of the night, and then Sonja and Kenny arrived.

"Hi, you guys. Why are you standing outside?"

"We're waiting for Merrick to answer the door."

Sonja reached over and rang the bell. "She probably didn't hear you knock." We waited another few minutes, and there was still no answer.

Janel and Mandy arrived. By then the front porch was jam-packed with mothers and babies. "What's going on?" Janel asked.

"Merrick hasn't answered the door yet."

"Well," Sonja said. "This is crazy. Do we have the wrong day?"

Just then the door opened, and there stood Merrick, her blonde hair wrapped up in a towel. It looked as if she'd been taking a shower. She looked put out that we'd all arrived on time, which I thought was odd because she was the one who had invited us.

"Could someone please help me with Bobby while I dry my hair?" I lifted her son out of her arms, and with Jill on one hip and Bobby on the other, I moved into the house along with the others.

The place was gorgeous, like a designer showcase, and it was spotless. The entrance floor was shiny white marble and a beautiful crystal chandelier hung from the ceiling. Pink and lavender flowers were arranged in a crystal vase and a beautiful photograph of her newborn son stood next to it. A huge ornate mirror hung over the table, making the entrance look larger than it actually was, and reflected in it was the all-white living room with a large painting of Merrick and her husband on one wall. Next to the white marble fireplace hung another oil painting of Merrick, seated in a beautiful chair with her husband standing behind her. He was young-looking and trim with black hair. Both were smiling.

We were ushered into the family room, which was spacious. Every piece of furniture was white or light grey, the tables were glass, and the lamps were crystal with lovely matching shades. One table had another vase of fresh flowers in the center and a large designer bookcase against one wall.

There was not one toy in sight.

We all oohed and aahed over Merrick's beautiful home, and Sonja whispered, "This looks like a model home, as if no one lives here.

Merrick announced she had to finish some business and excused herself, and we watched her walk out of the room. "What if one of our kids spits up on this nice white carpet?" Sonja asked.

"I have my quilt in the car," I said. "I'll get it."

I laid the quilt on the lush white carpet, and one by one we put our babies down. When Merrick returned she stared at the quilt. "Why did you do that, Ava?"

"I didn't want the babies to spit up on your lovely white carpet."

She smiled. "That's a wonderful idea." I was relieved. But she still stood there with the towel around her head.

"Ava, will you start the coffee?"

That took me by surprise. "Sure," I said. The other women stared at me.

"I'll go dry my hair, now," Merrick said. "You'll find everything in the kitchen."

Janel said she would watch Jill and Bobby while I made the coffee, so I reached into my diaper bag and pulled out a few toys to keep them busy.

I walked into Merrick's immaculate kitchen and caught my breath. The countertops were black granite, the cupboards were a beautiful, pristine white. I found the mugs and the coffeemaker, and finally found the coffee in the freezer of all places. I opened it very carefully to avoid making a mess, then I heard Merrick yell from the back of the house. "Ava, there's a box of brownie mix in the pantry if you want to make them."

I was flabbergasted. *I* should make the brownies? The women started to whisper among themselves, and from the looks on Sonja's and Ruthanne's faces I could see they didn't think this was funny. I overheard Ruthanne whisper, "We were invited here. She should at least have put the coffee on."

"Maybe," I said. "But now the coffee *is* on and brewing." I picked up Jill and shook a rattle at Bobby and Mandy until Merrick came back. All eyes were on her; we were all perplexed by her treatment of us.

"What?" she said loudly.

I watched some of the ladies try to keep their mouths shut. Ruthanne didn't.

"If you couldn't be ready for us today," she said, "you should have let *me* host the group."

Merrick raised her perfectly tweezed eyebrows and looked straight at her. "I had a really rough morning," she said tersely.

I stood up. "Merrick, let me help you with the coffee." I followed her into the kitchen and she turned to me. "I do not like Ruthanne," she blurted. "Kick her out of the baby group."

I lowered my voice. "Merrick," I said as calmly as I could, "maybe she had a bad morning, too."

"Well, she's rude and I won't take much more of her."

I took a tray of coffee and mugs out to the family room and prayed that no one would drip anything on the white carpet. That would definitely cause a problem. I noticed that all the women had gathered on the quilt with their babies, and I didn't care if anything was spilled on that.

Taylor started to talk to Merrick about her beautiful home and everyone else just listened. We heard each and every detail of how Merrick and her husband had built the house and had a professional decorator come in to arrange their furniture. Evidently this was one of three homes they had previously purchased and remodeled in their 10 years of marriage.

Sonja's mouth dropped open. "You have already moved three times?"

We listened in stunned silence as Merrick explained, then turned the conversation to her father, who was very ill. She sat on the corner of the quilt and kept twisting the big diamond ring on her finger. "I had to hire a nurse to help my father, who has dementia. He ran away from home last night." Merrick's head drooped.

I looked at her. "It must be hard to watch your father decline

When she heard this, we set aside her bad behavior earlier. Merrick obviously had her hands full taking care of both a newborn and her ailing father. I felt sorry for her. Any one of us could find ourselves in her shoes. She went on to say, "I was out last night at three o'clock looking for my father; he just walked out of the house. We finally found him at a gas station a mile away. I spent all morning on the phone, getting more help in my parents' home."

"Oh, Merrick, you should have called off baby group," I said quietly. Now I understood where her mind had been.

We stayed for almost three hours, talking about husbands, children, even religious beliefs. At one point Merrick was having a heated discussion with Taylor about divorced couples, and the two lapsed into whispers. I caught only a few words: "…so what? That happened when you were younger." And then Merrick intoned, "Don't tell anyone."

Ruthanne poked and prodded about money; Janel was sweet and sincere; and Taylor was the scholar who tried to find out where everyone had gone to college. When she got to Ruthanne, Taylor said, "Oh, you mean you went to junior college."

"It's still college," Ruthanne retorted.

Sonja and I tried to ease the focus away from over-personal conversations and gently reminded each other this was, after all, just a baby group. We certainly didn't need college degrees to be part of the discussions.

Janel changed the subject. "I'll host baby group next week." She told us where she lived and gave us directions. As we were getting up to leave Merrick said, "I am sorry to have kept you all waiting at the front door this morning. I was on the phone about my father."

"Don't worry about it," I said. "It's fine."

That night around the dinner table I asked my family, "What are the chances all those women belong to our parish? It's interesting that they're all Catholic."

"Why is that so interesting, Mom?" Gina asked.

"Oh, I don't know. Except for Taylor Carter, I haven't seen any of them at church. Actually, Taylor and Merrick Shoemaker are Eucharist ministers. You'd think I would have noticed that."

"They probably go to church at a different time," my husband explained.

I told my family about the lovely home Merrick lived in and that there was no sign that a baby lived there. And then I told them how she had asked me to make the coffee and bake some brownies. When I got to the part about her father escaping at three o'clock in the morning, James looked at me. "It can be really tough when your loved one's health declines."

"She was obviously upset from the night before. Merrick even asked me to kick Ruthanne out of the baby group. Ruthanne was just rude to Merrick. And when Merrick explained what had happened you would think Ruthanne would have understood."

My husband's gaze went up to the ceiling. "Did you kick her out?"

"Of course not. Merrick was just having a bad day." No sooner had I said this than the phone rang. It was Ruthanne. Her voice was high and tense.

"Ava, Merrick Shoemaker should be kicked out of the baby group!"

"Why? You heard what an awful night she had the night before."

"She wasn't ready for all of us this morning, and I've already talked to everyone in the group. She needs to go."

"Wait a minute. You called everyone in the group?"

"Well, yes."

"Ruthanne," I said gently. "Merrick just had a bad day, that's all. The next baby group will be at Janel's house, and I hope you'll be there."

"I'll think about it," she snapped. I hung up the phone and looked at James in disbelief. He came up behind me and wrapped his arms around me. "I heard your conversation. You handled that well."

"Sheesh, James, this is just a baby group! Ruthanne wants me to kick Merrick out."

"Did you tell her that Merrick wants *her* kicked out?"

"Of course not."

"Good. Keep it that way, Ava."

"I'm sure I'm going to get more phone calls."

"Maybe," James murmured. "They're acting like teenagers."

I had just started the dinner dishes when the phone rang again. This time it was Janel.

"Ava, I wouldn't even bother you about this baby group nonsense, but I thought you should know that Ruthanne just called me. She wants to vote you out of being the baby group organizer."

"Me! No, I haven't heard that." *My, my. Maybe I need to keep an eye on Ruthanne.*

"Janel, Merrick just had a bad night, and honestly if people don't want to come to a baby group, they don't have to."

"So, I'll see you next Wednesday?" she said. "I'll make sure to open the door on time."

"I wouldn't miss it for anything. I'm really interested in seeing what happens next." We both laughed.

"Ava? Would you bring your lovely quilt for the babies to lie on?"

"Sure, Janel. I'll launder it and put it in the car."

I wondered what would happen at the next baby group.

The following morning Taylor called. "Ava, I tried to call you last night, but the phone was busy. What's going on with the baby group?"

"What do you mean?"

"This whole thing about Ruthanne and Merrick."

"It's going to be fine. No one needs to come to this baby group if they feel the least bit uncomfortable."

"You mean you're going to stand for that kind of behavior?"

"Merrick just had a bad day," I said. "For God's sake, she was up in the middle of the night, taking care of her father."

"Hmmmm," was all she said.

I hung up thinking these women were making something out of nothing. When the phone rang again it was James, reminding me of dinner out at The Bistro that night. Before we ended the conversation I asked, "What's the best way to handle a few women in the baby group who have power issues? By not saying anything, right?"

"Probably. But if they get out of hand, watch out."

I knew exactly what he meant.

That night my husband and I entertained out-of-town guests at The Bistro. Before dinner was served I excused myself to go to the ladies' room and just happened to walk past a corner booth and glance at the couple sitting there very close to each other. The man was touching the woman's short dark hair and bringing her face to his. I felt like an intruder, so I turned my head away.

But as I passed the booth I heard a woman's distinctive voice, a low, musical voice that sounded familiar. I hesitated, then glanced back and saw Taylor from the baby group. I continued to the ladies' room thinking I would stop and say hello on my way back, but when I returned I noticed the man next to Taylor had wavy blond hair tucked behind his ears, blue eyes, and a dimple when he smiled. Taylor's husband had dark hair and brown eyes.

They had eyes only for each other and didn't notice me at all. The last thing I wanted to do was interrupt a romantic dinner Taylor was having with someone other than her husband. Maybe he was her brother? But a brother and sister would not behave that way.

Later, when I turned to get my wrap from the back of my chair I saw Taylor and the man hugging and kissing at the front entrance. Taylor put her head on his shoulder, then their eyes locked and they kissed again. Then he opened the restaurant door and they both disappeared into the night.

I was ready to burst with this information! In the car, I turned to James. "You would not believe who I saw inside the restaurant."

"Who?"

"Taylor, from the baby group."

"Oh. You should have told me. I would have gone over to say hello."

"I don't think she would have liked that. In fact, I hid myself when I realized it was her."

"He looked at me out of the corner of his eye. "Why?"

"Because she wasn't with Brandon, her husband. She was with someone else, and they were definitely making out."

"Are you sure? It was dark in the restaurant."

"I'm sure."

"Ava, you can't say anything about this, you do know that?"

"Yes, I know that. But wow, this is terrible for Brandon. And she has a baby at home! What is she thinking?"

My husband just shook his head, and I sighed. He was right. I would need to keep what I'd seen to myself. And I hated to keep secrets.

Between Friends

Jill and I were getting to know Janel and her little girl, Megan, outside of baby group. Today we were going to walk downtown with our children and have lunch out. We met in a downtown parking lot.

Getting the stroller out of the back of my mini-van I saw Janel's car pull into the parking garage. We had the same car and the same type of stroller, and we both had older children. We got along famously.

As we were feeding our babies their bottles, Janel suddenly said, "Did you hear about Merrick?"

I flinched inside. "I don't think so."

"I'm not sure I should say anything, but I overheard her talking to Taylor at the last baby group."

"What about?"

"Evidently Merrick works from home."

"After all that fuss she made about mothers staying at home? Are you sure about this?"

"Yes," Janel said.

"What kind of work does she do?"

"She manages home rentals for her family."

"I wonder why she didn't just come right out and tell us?"

"I don't know."

"Boy, she has her hands full, working full-time with an infant and caring for her father."

"And," Janel continued, "there's something else. Sonja and Ruthanne are not getting along. Have you noticed?"

"How could I not notice? Time will tell if they stick with the baby group or not."

* * *

Janel hosted the next baby group, and I couldn't help wondering what surprises were in store this time. I rang her doorbell and she opened it immediately.

"That was fast," I said with a laugh. "I barely rang your bell!"

"Ava, thank goodness you're here! I've been standing by the door for the last fifteen minutes to make sure I opened it quickly. I don't want to keep anyone waiting, like we did at Merrick's."

"Sure," I said with a nod. "I understand."

"Will you watch the door while I pour the coffee?"

"Janel, I don't think you need to pour the coffee just yet. Why not wait for everyone to get here?"

"I'm not taking any chances," she said.

Janel lived in a gated community on the east side of town. Her entryway took you straight into the living area, which had a long sofa and matching chairs across the room with a table in between. A beautiful Oriental tapestry hung on the wall with wall sconces on either side. Toys were scattered on the other side of the room, along with a playhouse for her older son.

I put Megan and Jill on my quilt and took out my camera to capture the two of them together.

One by one the ladies arrived, and Janel quickly opened the door each time. No sooner had they placed their babies on my quilt than a cup of coffee was in their hands.

Ruthanne brought a new woman, Samantha, a tall woman in her late twenties who had a daughter named Alice. Janel shook Samantha's hand and welcomed her, but when Janel asked me to help her with coffee in the kitchen, she blurted, "The nerve of Ruthanne, bringing someone to the group that I don't even know!"

"I had no idea she would do something like that," I said.

"Do we have to invite Samantha to the group from now on?"

"Let's just play it by ear and see what we think about her first." I took the coffee tray back into the living room and kept my eye on Ruthanne and Samantha.

We talked mostly about our children and the newest place to buy baby clothes. "Jill's formula stains both her clothing and mine," I said, "so I need to keep a few new outfits in her closet." A few of the other mothers agreed, saying they were also bottle-feeding.

And then Ruthanne spoke up. "It's a shame you don't nurse your child."

Everyone stared at her.

"Ruthanne," I said quietly, "nursing may not be for everyone."

"It's just a cop-out," she snapped. "And it's bad for the child in the long run."

The room fell silent. I was fuming inside. How dare she tell me what I was doing was right or wrong? Finally Janel changed the subject.

"Did any of you register for the Mommy and Me class?"

While the ladies discussed it, I followed Janel into her kitchen for more coffee. "I can't believe Ruthanne keeps putting her foot in her mouth," she complained.

"I know," I admitted. "And I'm not happy about her telling those of us who bottle-feed that we're doing it wrong."

"Are you going to invite her back to the baby group?"

"It's not up to me," I answered.

"Sure it is. You put the group together, right?"

"Janel, I'm not kicking anyone out. I have a feeling we don't know that full story about Ruthanne yet."

"I don't think we know the full story about any of these women," Janel whispered.

I was wondering what she meant by that when she leaned close and murmured, "I saw you and James at The Bistro last Thursday night."

I looked at her in surprise, and then she said something else. "I saw Taylor Carter there, too. With a man." Her eyes were smiling as we walked back into her living room. I couldn't wait for today's baby group to be over with.

The ladies all decided that the next group would meet at Taylor's house. "You all have my phone number," she said, then reached in her purse and pulled out printed directions to her home. We were impressed at how organized she was.

I stayed to help Janel clean up. I also wanted to find out what she thought about Taylor and that man at The Bistro last Thursday. "Spill the beans," I said. "What exactly did you see at the restaurant that night?"

Janel smiled. "All week I've had a hard time not talking to you about it, Ava. I was waiting until I saw Taylor's husband before I said anything, and then this Sunday I saw the whole family at church. She introduced me to her husband, Brandon. The guy she was with at The Bistro was not her husband."

I shook my head. "What gave you the clue last Thursday?"

"The way she was hanging all over the guy. Also, when they were being seated I heard him ask Taylor if her husband was really out of town and for how long. Watching her made me feel uneasy, so I held my menu up in front of my face. What do you think is going on?"

"I have no idea, but I feel awful for Brandon."

"It may not be what it looks like," Janel said. "Rich told me to stay out of it."

"So did James."

"This can only end badly for someone," she said with a sigh.

We both agreed.

Different in Every Way but Love

Right before the next baby group meeting Janel called me. "I can't wait to see what Ruthanne will say this time. I'll pick you and Jill up." I couldn't wait, either, but I said nothing.

Wednesday arrived. On Taylor's porch, Janel whispered, "Keep your ears open for any clues about her male friend."

"I'm sure she won't say anything," I said.

"Don't bet on it."

We rang the doorbell and Taylor quickly opened her door, looking trim in her black slacks, and hugged us both. Her house was a large two-story structure, and her entry had a traditional look. She had lovely taste in colors and fabrics; the chair next to her piano looked like an antique, covered in a cream-colored fabric with the wood on the arms and legs carved in a beautiful pattern."

"This chair is beautiful," I said.

"Yes, it's been in our family for many years."

Photos of her and Brandon covered the walls, and there was one family photograph that struck me; everyone in it had dark hair and brown eyes. All ten of them!

"Where does your family live?" I asked.

"They're all back in New Hampshire. I'm the only one who's moved. It was hard to leave those I love."

I saw Janel's eyebrows go up and I wondered what she was thinking.

"Yes," I said, "it must be very hard to move away from your family and your job and have a new baby, too."

Taylor shook her head and looked rather sad. We ended up in her kitchen, which had light brown cupboards and light hardwood floors. The walls were off-white and along the back door were drapes with a hint of blue. Outside there was a large lap pool surrounded by lovely green plants with yellow, daisy-like flowers.

The women arrived, and Ruthanne had brought her young friend Samantha again. "I had no idea Samantha would be coming," Taylor remarked out loud.

I felt bad for Samantha. She was quite tall and very thin. Her daughter, Alice, was a good six months older than all the other babies and was already standing up. "My husband is in the beverage industry," she volunteered. "Greg is a short man and he likes everything to be perfect."

I thought that was a very odd way to describe one's spouse. Samantha then spied Taylor's family photos on the wall. "Hey, Taylor, who is Megan's father?" she blurted. "Everyone has dark brown hair and eyes, and just look at little Megan! She is blonde and blue-eyed."

Janel and I watched Taylor's reaction. She blushed. "That's my little girl," she said quickly. "Different in every way but love."

Janel's gaze met mine across the room. Taylor didn't say that Brandon was the father. In fact, she didn't point to anyone in the photograph as being Megan's father.

The doorbell rang and Taylor went to answer it to find Ruthanne standing there with Sonja and Kenny. Taylor rushed to get more coffee, and the photo moment passed.

A few hours went by, and then Taylor announced in her low voice that she had prepared a casual lunch for anyone who wanted to stay. I went into the kitchen to see if I could help.

"Ava, I would love it if you got the plates out of that cupboard and put them on the table." She then had me cut up fruit for the salad. "Just put it in this bowl, and please put it on the table. Now, you can get the silverware, over there." When everything was ready, we both walked into the family room and Taylor announced, "Lunch is served. Please help yourselves."

During lunch, Sonja finger-combed her sun-bleached hair as if she were nervous and finally offered to host the next baby group. "Ava, could you bring your lovely quilt?"

"Sure." I was happy that my quilt was becoming a valued part of the group.

While I was putting my plate in the sink, Taylor came up behind me. "Would you like to go with me and Megan to a new gym class just for babies next Tuesday? I have two free tickets for a friend and a child."

"Sounds like fun," I said. I wondered if anyone else would be invited, but I didn't ask. On my way out the door with Janel, Taylor tapped me on the shoulder and whispered, "I'll call you about Tuesday."

Janel stared at her, then at me, and continued on out the door. In the car, she asked, "Where are you and Taylor going on Tuesday?"

"Some gym class for babies. Do you want to come?"

"I wasn't invited."

"Let me go to the first one, and I'll bring you and Mandy in for the next one." I could see she felt left out. "Janel, we have time before we pick up the older kids; do you want to stop for coffee?"

She grinned. "Sure."

Over coffee Janel asked if I'd taken a good look at Taylor's blue-eyed daughter in the family photograph. "Not really," I said. "What did you see?"

"Megan looks nothing like anyone in that family."

I looked at her. "Today I noticed Megan's dimple; it's on her right cheek. That guy Taylor was with at the restaurant had an identical dimple. You don't suppose...?"

Janel shook her head and again reminded me it might not be what it looked like.

Sonja's House

The morning Sonja was hosting the group I was the first one to arrive. Even though we had known each other for many years, I had never been to her home but had met her at the country club to play tennis. Her skin was always deeply tanned.

Her home was absolutely magnificent. And huge, at the end of a long driveway with green shrubbery and trees that blocked out nearby houses. Baby toys were scattered all over the spacious living room. I put Jill down on the quilt and Sonja put Kenny right next to her.

"They're adorable, aren't they?" I said. I took out my camera, snapped a photo, and promised her a copy.

When Janel and Mandy, arrived I let them in. "Sonja's in the kitchen getting the coffee," I explained.

"Wow," Janel whispered. "This house is really big!"

Sonja poked her head in. "Hello, Janel."

"Sonja, do you need any help in the kitchen?"

She laughed. "Only if you can make brownies from scratch." When she returned to the living room, Merrick, Taylor, and Samantha were sitting on the quilt playing with the babies. Behind

Sonja was a woman in a maid's uniform with a plate of brownies. I'd thought she was joking about the brownies! These brownies *were* homemade, but not by Sonja.

Then Ruthanne came in. The first thing she said was, "Whoa, Sonja, your home is spectacular!"

Sonja just said, "Thank you."

Today Ruthanne wore a very short navy blue dress with red buttons down the back and a pair of bright red heels. She carried a red Prada handbag. Very carefully she removed her shoes and sat down on the quilt. Ruthanne was the only one of us who dressed up for baby group. I wondered if she ever wore jeans and casual shoes.

"Let me give you a tour of the house," Sonja offered. "Mildred, my maid, has child care training; she will watch all the infants." As we started to follow her, Janel and I scooped up our babies and carried them with us.

"Mitch and I just hired another nanny," Sonja continued. "She starts next week. Our last nanny didn't work out; she couldn't speak fluent Korean."

Janel and I just looked at each other.

The living room was sparse because, Sonja admitted, she couldn't decide how to decorate it. But all the other rooms were decorated to the hilt. I had never seen so many original paintings, and the windows had blinds on the inside of the panes that opened and closed electronically. The basement had been turned into a music studio. Evidently Sonja and Mitch were music fans; many different instruments were lined up along the wall.

Upstairs we walked to the end of a long hall and there was an elevator! We all got in and it took us up to the second floor, where four bedrooms were decorated in different color schemes. Each one had its own full bath and sitting area. When we reached the master suite I stared in disbelief. A series of portraits of Sonja wearing lingerie hung over the king-sized bed.

Again Janel and I just looked at each other. I felt I was intruding on Sonja's privacy. "Those photos are for her husband's eyes only," Janel whispered.

We walked past the master bathroom and there, hanging on a wall, was a huge photograph of a much younger Sonja, in the nude. I saw Janel cover Megan's eyes as we passed. Sonja was so busy talking about the furniture and her travels that she didn't notice our reactions to the nude photograph.

On our way back down to the main floor, Sonja announced, "Mildred and I planned a lovely lunch for you all today. We will serve it on the back patio."

As we walked back down the long hallway toward the living room I couldn't help noticing the photographs on either side. All were of Sonja or Mitch—the two of them on a balloon ride with the French Alps below; Mitch in the front seat of an airplane Sonja said they bought ten years ago. "The new plane is much nicer," she said. On the other side of the wall was a photo of Sonja in a race car.

"I came in fourth," she said in my ear.

"You race cars, Sonja?"

"I love to drive fast."

I stopped at the next photo of an overgrown jungle scene of what looked like the Amazon, which Sonja confirmed. She and Mitch were in a boat. She then told us that she and Mitch had traveled the world, knowing that when they had a child they would have to stay home for a year.

Only a year? I thought. But then I didn't have a live-in maid and a nanny. Later I discovered that Sonja had her own chauffeur.

Janel leaned close and whispered, "I wonder if she plans on home-schooling and will hire a teacher to live in?"

I said nothing.

"What kind of doctor is her husband?"

"One that is very successful," I whispered back.

The baby group conversation today was more about Sonja's house than babies. Then it was time for lunch. Sonja had her fine china out on the back porch table, which was set with pretty linens and a centerpiece of fresh flowers. The maid served us, and the babies lay on my quilt under the shade of a beautiful Japanese maple tree. We had shrimp for lunch with a tasty salad and delicious iced tea.

Suddenly Ruthanne blurted, "Sonja, what kind of money does it take to run this kind of household?"

Everyone stared at her. Instinctively I knew this would offend Sonja, and Merrick and Taylor both opened their mouths to say something, but didn't.

Sonja just smiled at Ruthanne. "I wouldn't ask you how much it costs to run *your* home, Ruthanne. Kindly do me the same favor."

Ruthanne put on a sulky face and whispered something to Merrick, who shushed her right up. "Mind your own business and enjoy this lovely lunch."

One by one the babies started waking up, and someone said, "Sonja, we've had a wonderful day today. Thank you for hosting the baby group." We all raised our iced tea glasses to her.

Samantha then spoke up shyly. "I will host the next baby group. But I just want you to know that my home is nowhere near as grand as this one."

No one said a word. *None* of our homes could compare to this one! Sonja spoke up first.

"I am sure we will all have a lovely time at your home, Samantha."

When we started to leave, Mildred had a tray of brownies wrapped in foil for each of us, with a piece of Godiva chocolate on top. What a nice touch!

Janel and I were the last to leave, and we both thanked Sonja again for having us.

"I am so glad we met up in the grocery store that day, Ava," she said. "I look forward to this group every week. When I met you it was the week we let our nanny go, and I was a wreck. You threw me this wonderful lifeline."

I was flabbergasted. "Well," I managed, "we're happy to have you in the group."

"Let's go get coffee at the Coffee Bean," Janel said as we walked out. When I reached my car I glanced back at Sonja's home. She was standing in her doorway, just looking at us. I wondered if she had overheard us making coffee plans. I buckled Jill in her car seat and went back to the front door where Sonja stood.

"Janel and I are going to the Coffee Bean. Do you and Kenny want to join us?"

Her face lit up. "Oh, I would love to go! I'll meet you there." She sounded so excited I had to laugh.

Janel was already seated at the Coffee Bean when I told her we needed to grab another chair for Sonja. She looked at me in surprise. "She overheard us making plans," I explained. "I felt it was the right thing to do."

At that moment Sonja walked through the door with Kenny. "I hope I am not intruding," she said quietly.

"Don't be silly. We're happy to have you here with us. Both Janel and I have a few hours before we have to pick up our older children; we like to hang out here and talk."

Sonja smiled. "The two of you look so comfortable together. Friendship is a special gift," she said slowly. She paused. "I haven't been so lucky with friends." She went on to tell us how her best friend had died of cancer last year. "I had been trying for ten years to have a child, and I ended up needing in-vitro fertilization. My friend used to take me to the doctor. I was at number four try when she had a mammogram and they found a lump. The doctors didn't give her a good prognosis, so Mitch and I flew her to the Mayo

Clinic and got the top doctors to look at her. But she died just a few months before I delivered Kenny. She never saw him."

Janel and I were silent. I put my hand over Sonja's, and just then Kenny started to cry. Sonja took a bottle out of her diaper bag.

Janel stood up. "What kind of coffee do you want, Sonja?"

"Regular coffee with room for cream, please."

"Same for me," I said. I held onto Mandy while Janel got three coffees.

"You are so lucky to have Janel for a good friend," Sonja said. "And she is lucky to have you, Ava. You are kind-hearted, and I can see you are a good mother. I hope I can be like you."

"Wow. I'm learning how to parent as I go, Sonja. But thank you for your kind words."

"Sonja," Janel asked, "how are you feeling now that Kenny is here?"

Sonja sighed. "Overwhelmed. I hired a nanny to help during the night hours and I have Mildred to help with my huge house during the day. I had no idea that my sweet little baby would change my life so much."

Sonja was just like any one of us, I thought. She was going through the grief of losing her best friend and she was tired from being a new mother. She was trying to do what was right for her family under pressure.

"When your friend died, did you get any counseling?" I asked gently. "It sounds like the two of you were very close."

"Instead of counseling, Mitch decided we needed to buy this big house and to travel. But I loved my old house! It was in an old neighborhood and I could always go next door and get some sugar if I ran out. This neighborhood, they expect you to send your servant to the store. No one talks in the driveway or walks their own dogs. I hate my new life."

"Sonja, have you talked this over with your husband?"

"He wants all of this stuff," she said. "We are in two different places right now."

I started to feel really sorry for her. Our coffee time flew by and we hadn't solved any problems, but both Janel and I told Sonja to call us; we could meet for coffee any time. She loved that idea, and we set up another time for coffee and to just talk next week after baby group. When we got up to leave, Sonja turned to me. "Thank you, guys, for listening. It means the world to me."

We hugged her goodbye. "See you next week at Samantha's," I said. "And Sonja, please do call me any time you want to talk."

That night at dinner I told James about the house with the elevator. "That must have been some place," he said.

"James, Sonja is really nice. She's just like any of us; she just owns a very expensive home and a few airplanes parked someplace—at the airport, I guess."

He chuckled. "Don't tell me she has maids, too?"

I nodded. "Yes."

"I figured," he said. "Sounds like your sister."

I thought for a minute. "You're right. Sonja could sense that I was not impressed by her 'things.' Money doesn't make the person."

Who Was She With?

The following Sunday at Mass I saw Taylor and her husband and their daughter, Megan. The Eucharist minister was Merrick Shoemaker, and her family was sitting in the front pew. I also saw Janel and her family, and Ruthanne and Jon were sitting on the far side.

After the service I overheard James ask one of the men if he wanted to play tennis sometime. I turned around and there were Sonja and Mitch and Kenny. What a small world!

The following week I got a phone call from Samantha. "Ava," she said hesitantly, "is there a rule that we have to host the baby group in our homes?"

"No, not at all. We can go to Oak Tree Park, or you can come to my house if you like."

"You see, Greg, my husband, works from home and he can't be disturbed."

"No problem. What would you like to do?"

"Let's go to the park. I'll call everyone."

At the end of the day, Ruthanne called, loudly complaining that baby group was being changed and maybe we should kick Samantha out because she was not complying with the rules.

"What rules are those, Ruthanne? We never said we had to host the baby group in our homes. The park would be just fine, like the first time I hosted the group."

I could tell by her voice that Ruthanne was upset. "Well," she said. "I called everyone to tell them it will be at my house, not at the park."

"Excuse me? Tell me you didn't really do that. It's Samantha's turn, and we are meeting at the park. I will personally call everyone and let them know she is having the baby group at Oak Tree Park."

"Ava, you're making a big mistake here."

"You're making something out of nothing, Ruthanne. Please leave it alone."

Ruthanne hung up.

I called everyone. Janel offered her home again. Taylor thought we should vote Ruthanne out of the group for being destructive. Sonja thought I handled it well. Samantha was in tears about not being able to host it at her home, and I told her not to worry.

"Ava, could I borrow your quilt for the baby group?"

"Sure. Anything else? I have two large thermoses for coffee and a lot of extra cups."

"That would be wonderful. You are very thoughtful, Ava."

"We're here to help each other out, not make more problems."

Merrick didn't answer her phone, so I left her a message.

That night over dinner I told James what was happening with the group. He said it looked like there were a few hens in the group who liked total control.

"I know. I'm trying my best to stay neutral."

James then said, "We're hosting another business group on Thursday at Le Fleur restaurant."

"I'll put it on the calendar. I wonder if I will run into anyone else like I did at The Bistro?"

* * *

Thursday night came and we were the first to arrive at Le Fleur. This time on my way out of the powder room I saw pretty, blonde Merrick sitting at a table with Brandon Carter! I looked for Brandon's wife but didn't see her. What were Merrick and Brandon doing there together? Was one of the husbands messing around with another woman in the same baby group?

I ducked my head, and when I returned to my table I turned ever so slightly to see exactly what was going on at Merrick's table.

It *was* Brandon! And he had his arm around Merrick's shoulder. She moved close to him and then there was a kiss. *Oh, my God, they're having an affair!* I tried to look away, but I wanted to see more in spite of myself. I watched Merrick get up to go to the restroom. Did I dare go, too?

I excused myself and again went to the ladies room. I was standing at the doorway inside the restroom when I heard someone in the first stall. I stood and waited, and Merrick finally came out. When her eyes met mine she blushed scarlet. "Ava, what are you doing here?"

"James and I are entertaining some business associates tonight."

"So you came to Le Fleur," she said, her voice quiet.

"Are you celebrating a special occasion, Merrick?

She walked to the sink and said nothing, just washed her hands. I could see her face and her eyes; she was trying to come up with a story. "Oh, no, it's not what it looks like, Ava."

"What does it look like?" I asked.

"Brandon and I are…planning a surprise birthday party for Taylor."

That made all the sense in the world, coming to a fancy restaurant an hour away from where they live to plan a birthday party. "Where is the party?"

"At her home."

"Where are Robert and your kids tonight?"

Her face flushed. "Oh, they're at home. Ava, I would love to stay and chat, but I need to get back to the table."

"Right. I'll see you at baby group this week?"

"Yes." And that's all she said. Back at my table I noticed Brandon and Merrick hurrying to leave. Brandon took a long look at me, and Merrick did, too. They both looked embarrassed. I felt real sadness for each of their families.

When James and I walked to our car I told him. "You wouldn't believe who I saw in the restaurant tonight."

"Ava, you ran into someone the *last* time we went out."

"Yes, I did. And it happened again."

"Who was it this time?"

"Merrick Shoemaker. And she was with Brandon Carter, Taylor's husband. I went to the restroom and ran into Merrick; I'd already seen Brandon at her table."

"Don't say a word," James advised. "I wouldn't touch this with a ten-foot pole!"

"Baby group is getting awkward. Two of them are having affairs with each other's husbands, and they are both Eucharist ministers at church!"

"I feel sad for what this can do to their marriages," he said.

"I feel bad for seeing it. I wished I hadn't."

James hugged me. "You need to send out a memo to the baby group," he said with a laugh. "Tell them where and when we're eating out, so this doesn't happen again."

Mind Your Own Business

I made coffee and poured it in the thermoses, then got out the quilt for the baby group and put it in the bottom of Jill's stroller. When I got to the park, I met Samantha on the curvy part of the trail.

"I hope I didn't stir up any commotion about having baby group here at the park," she said.

"No, don't think twice about it. I love coming to the park. It's a beautiful summer morning and we can all use the fresh air."

Taylor Carter arrived, and she was not in a good mood. "Ava, I have to talk to you." Her usually low, pleasant voice was clipped.

I looked up at her. "Okay."

"Over here, please." I walked over to a tree with her. She looked down on me and said sharply, "How dare you tell my husband and me how to run our lives!"

"What?"

"You know what I'm talking about. Brandon was at a business meeting with a colleague last Thursday night, and he said you interrupted and made a snide remark about me."

"Wait a minute," I protested. "What colleague was he with?"

"Frank Summervale, his boss from Connecticut."

Oh, my God. Brandon had gone home and told Taylor a lie. He wasn't with his boss from Connecticut; he was with Merrick Shoemaker! "I have no idea what you're talking about," I said. "I was entertaining a business group with James at Le Fleur. I didn't speak to Brandon at all."

Her face turned red. "Are you sure?"

"Of course I'm sure. I didn't speak to Brandon." I wasn't going to tell her that I *had* spoken with Merrick Shoemaker, though.

"I'm sorry, Ava. I've been on edge lately. Brandon seems to be going out of town and out to dinner a lot lately, and I'm not coping well. Megan is such a handful I could just scream."

She was also juggling her own affair, and that must be taxing on her nerves. But I kept quiet.

"Ava, could you meet me for coffee sometime?"

"Sure." I wondered what she wanted to talk about, surely not her own affair? Her marriage must be a mess at this point. "What about tomorrow morning?" I suggested. "Why don't you come over to my house?"

After she agreed, we walked back to the group; they had assembled all our infants on the quilt and I brought out some extra teething toys for them to play with. Today the conversation ranged from signs of teething to what to do about going back to work.

Ruthanne was already back working part-time, and she was not adjusting well. As cute as her baby Jon was, he was not sleeping well. She was exhausted and wanted to know what we all did to get our babies to go to sleep at a reasonable hour. She was worried that he was the only infant who woke up in the middle of the night.

"That's normal," I said. "In fact, all our babies are waking up at some point during the night. And as far as getting him to sleep, just get into the same routine at night, like bathing him and not being too loud and nursing him right before you lay him down. You might even see if you can get him to lie down by himself. That might be good in the long run."

Everyone else nodded in agreement.

"You mean you all bathe your kids every night?" Ruthanne asked.

"I do," I said. "It calms Jill down. But do whatever works for you."

Merrick spoke up. "I have this stuffed toy that you put in the microwave for thirty seconds. It's barely warm, and I put it on Bobby's tummy while I give him his last bottle. Puts him to sleep every time."

"Jill still stays in my bedroom," I confessed. "She pretty much sleeps until four in the morning."

"That's when Mandy wakes up," Janel said.

"Megan wakes up at three every morning," Taylor said. The doctor said she's gaining weight so well she should be sleeping more in the next few weeks. I hope that's true."

By that time we had all tried to solve the problems of sleeping babies and late night feedings, so we started to pack up and go home. Samantha had been very quiet, and I wondered what was going on with her.

"I'll see you tomorrow, Ava," Taylor said loudly. Everyone looked at us. I wished Taylor had kept our coffee arrangement between just the two of us. Janel and I walked out together, and Sonja caught up with us. "Are we going to Coffee Bean?"

"Sure," Janel said.

When I reached Coffee Bean, Janel and Sonja were deep in conversation. "What's new with you two this week?" I asked.

"Not that much," Janel said. "But Sonja has some bad news."

I looked at Sonja and waited. "Well," she said after a pause, "this is hard to explain, but I decided to take Kenny to a pediatric specialist. He's just not thriving like all of your children, and I noticed it."

I had no idea what she was talking about.

"I found out that Kenny has a heart problem," Sonja went on. "He needs surgery this month. The doctors feel he has an abnormality in his heart and they'll try to repair it. Mitch says we will go into the city to find the best surgeon."

I grabbed her hand and held it. "I am so sorry to hear this. How frightening for you both. If there's anything I can do, please let me know."

"Oh, thank you. I really appreciate it. I'd really like to keep this to ourselves until I know more about the prognosis. You know I had in-vitro fertilization, and I'm worried that something neurological could be going on."

"Sonja, did the doctor tell you that?"

"No, but now I am worrying about everything."

When we left we all hugged each other and agreed to meet again.

That evening, when James got home from work, I told him about little Kenny. "Do they need anything?" he asked.

"Mostly they need friendship," I said. "You might want to call Mitch and see if you can help."

"Okay, will do."

"James, Taylor was just terrible this morning. She said I had some nerve to barge in on Brandon's business meeting."

"What? What does that mean?"

"That's what I wanted to know. She has no idea that her husband is having an affair with Merrick Shoemaker, and Brandon has no idea his wife is having an affair with that man I saw at The Bistro that night. What a mess, huh?"

"Stay out of it, Ava."

"Don't worry, I intend to. There's nothing I can say anyway. What a terrible way to live!"

By the time I got Jill bathed and down for the night it was after 9 o'clock. I was pretty tired and then I suddenly remembered on the following day I was supposed to go with Taylor Carter and Megan to the gym class. I resolved not to spill any beans about what I had seen.

The following morning I arrived at Taylor's house to be told she had forgotten she had to telephone to see if Jill could join the class today. We took a chance, loaded the kids into their car seats, and went anyway. Taylor drove with one hand on the steering wheel and kept looking back at Megan in her car seat, which made me nervous. I kept an eye on the road and tried to keep myself from telling her how to drive.

Finally she turned to me. "What were you and James doing at the restaurant the other night, Ava?"

"We were entertaining some business associates." I looked at her out of the corner of my eye. "We entertain quite a bit for James's work."

"What a coincidence you were at the same place Brandon was."

I wasn't going to be the one to tell her Brandon was there with Merrick Shoemaker and not a work colleague. I kept my eyes on the road and listened to her go on and on about how much Brandon was traveling these days.

When we walked in the door of the gym I saw lots of colorful balls on mats for the infant to play with. Taylor registered Jill and me and then I looked around. Oh, there were Janel and Mandy sitting on a bench just taking their shoes off.

"I didn't invite Janel," Taylor whispered. I said nothing, but I did go over and give Janel and Mandy a hug. "Fancy meeting you guys here," I said with a smile.

Then I noticed Ruthanne walking in the front door with Jon. Again, Taylor whispered to me, "Looks like it's an extension of baby group today." She did not sound happy.

We all exchanged pleasantries and for the next hour listened to the instructor and played with the children. When it was time to leave I signed up for the following month. Ruthanne and Janel signed up, too.

After class all of us decided to go out to lunch. At the restaurant, Ruthanne started talking about her friend who had just found out her husband was having an affair. "You should have seen her crying her eyes out. I would never tell on anyone if I knew they were having an affair."

"Did you know her husband was having the affair?" Taylor asked.

Ruthanne nodded. "How awful," Taylor said. "How could you have kept that secret from your friend?"

Ruthanne looked straight at her. "There are things you just don't say when it involves your friends. Your friend could blame you for what happened."

"I would want to know," Taylor answered. I kept quiet and my gaze locked with Janel's. We both knew about Taylor and that man she'd had dinner with, but neither of us was about to say anything.

On the ride home Taylor said, "I want to know why Brandon would tell me you interrupted his business meeting the other night."

I was silent, struggling to think of what to say. Finally I blurted, "I have no idea why he would have said that." But I wondered what else he had said to Taylor to cover up his actions.

She began to tell me how she and Brandon were under a lot of stress with the move and everything. She kept changing lanes without looking first, and I gripped the seat of the car. Did she know in her heart what Brandon was doing? For that matter, did Brandon know what Taylor was doing with that other man I'd seen her with?

When she turned into her driveway I said quickly, "I have to get Jill home for her nap."

"Ava, before you leave, did you hear about little Kenny?"

"All I know is that Sonja said he needs heart surgery. I hope she knows we can help her out with meals while Kenny is recovering."

"I think she said she'd be coming to baby group next week, but we never said where it would meet. Isn't it Ruthanne's turn?"

Wine, Anyone?

The following week we met at Ruthanne's. I put my quilt down for the babies and then Ruthanne said Sonja had called that morning. The doctor had told her to keep Kenny away from other children until after his surgery. "She sounded very down about this whole thing."

"There has to be something we can do for her," I said. The rest of the group agreed. Except for Ruthanne.

"Well, she has a maid and a nanny. What more does she need?"

That sounded heartless. "I'm going to call her, see how she's doing," I said.

Ruthanne's house was much smaller than the others, but she had a fabulous touch in decorating. She had hardwood floors and overstuffed chairs and a large sofa in the family room, with a very large television. Photos of her family hung on all the walls.

Coffee was brewing and an applesauce cake sat on her countertop. Everyone was chatting away when Ruthanne offered us some wine. Taylor looked at me. I looked at Janel, and Merrick looked at Samantha. "No, thanks," Janel said. "It's a bit early to drink."

"It's six o'clock somewhere in the world," Ruthanne replied. "Cheers." I watched her take an already full glass out of her refrigerator.

Something was not quite right in Ruthanne's world.

That night over dinner I told James about what happened at baby group. "It was ten o'clock in the morning, and Ruthanne was drinking!"

"Does she do this all the time?" he asked.

"I honestly don't know. This is the first time I've ever seen her drink anything. No one has ever offered alcohol in the morning."

"Maybe this is an isolated instance."

Just then the phone rang. It was Janel. "I couldn't believe Ruthanne was drinking at baby group today!"

"She might be going through a rough patch," I said.

"Time will tell. I hope she's all right."

"Janel, we can set a good example for her, but that's pretty much all we can do."

When I hung up, James was still sitting on the sofa. "Do you think Ruthanne has a drinking problem?"

"I really don't know. She seemed fine when we first met, although she was very eager to know personal things about everyone."

"I wouldn't say anything, Ava."

I snuggled up to him and started to watch television when the phone rang again. This time it was Taylor.

"Ava, what are we going to do about Ruthanne?"

"What do you mean?" I knew exactly what she meant, but I hesitated to say anything.

"We're not going to condone drinking at baby group, are we?"

"Not in *our* homes. What she does in her own home is her business. She's never done that before," I pointed out.

"Maybe we need to kick her out of the group before it gets out of hand."

"I think we should wait and see what happens. Let's give it some time, Taylor. What if she's reaching out to us?"

"I have my own problems," she said. "I don't need her problems, too."

What a terrible reaction to someone who might need help!

"Ava," she said quickly, "Brandon just got home. I have to go."

When I returned to the living room, James motioned for me to sit beside him. "Ava, try not to get sucked into anyone else's drama."

I laid my head on his shoulder. "I won't."

My House

The week went by in a blur. Baby group was meeting at my house, and that morning I found myself rushing around doing some last-minute cleaning. It was a beautiful day outside, so I put the quilt on the grass in the back yard. Blooming roses lined the fence on one side and the grass was green and had been freshly cut.

Janel and Mandy were first to arrive, and then Taylor. "Your back yard looks like a park," she said in her low voice. "What a great place to have parties!"

I was keenly aware of Ruthanne when she arrived with Jon. "Your house is nice and homey, Ava," she said as she walked past me. I smelled alcohol. I escorted her out back to the quilt, but for some reason she sat in a chair away from everyone.

The doorbell rang and a nervous-looking Samantha stood there, along with Sonja and Kenny. I was happy Sonja had come, but at the same time I was worried about the doctor's orders for her not to be around the rest of us. "I called the doctor," she said. "I told him I was getting depressed from not being around my friends, so he said as long as you guys don't sneeze on Kenny or touch his hands, we should be fine." She went on to say "We had to prop the mattress in Kenny's crib at an angle so he can breathe easier."

Ruthanne was grinning. I asked why she was so happy.

"Well, I did something very out of the ordinary this weekend." She told us that her husband, Walter, has been coming in from a long business trip and how tired she was. She decided to greet him at the airport.

"Oh, that's nice, Ruthanne," I said.

She started to laugh. "What's so funny?" someone asked.

"I had my mother stay the night so Walter and I could have some alone time. I borrowed her full-length fur coat, and when I picked him up at the airport I didn't wear anything underneath it!"

We all gasped. Janel choked on her coffee. Samantha coughed. "You really drove all the way to the airport like that?"

Ruthanne had a twinkle in her eye. "It took a few drinks to get up the nerve to do it."

"Your mother knew you were doing that?" Taylor asked.

"God, no. I rented a hotel room and changed there, before I drove to the airport."

We were all speechless. Finally Sonja chuckled and said, "I am so glad I didn't miss this baby group today. This really took my mind off Kenny's surgery."

After that we started talking about who was starting on solid food and Kenny's surgery. Some of us offered to bring dinners to Sonja when her baby came home from the hospital.

Then Taylor turned to Samantha. "What happened to your leg?"

Samantha had a huge black-and-blue bruise on her thigh. She pulled her shorts down to cover it. "Oh, silly me. I ran into the corner of my dresser."

"Ouch," I said.

"It'll go away in a week or two," she remarked casually. I noticed that she wouldn't look at any of us.

When we started to leave, Ruthanne offered to help me clean up. Before I knew it she was tossing things into the garbage can under the kitchen sink.

That night after dinner I mentioned Ruthanne to James, and how I had smelled alcohol when she walked by. "Ava, unless you actually saw her dinking here at our home, you can't do anything about it. Did you see her drinking?"

"No, but I discovered two small empty vodka bottles in the kitchen garbage. They could only be Ruthanne's."

"You need to stay out of it."

"But what about her driving when she's under the influence?"

"Just make sure you always drive when she's in the car with you. Better yet, don't drive anywhere with her."

At that moment the phone rang. It was Janel. "Oh my gosh, Ava, could you ever do what Ruthanne did?"

"No. Positively not."

"Why did she keep her distance from everyone today?"

I didn't say anything and then tried to change the subject. "It was good to see Sonja, wasn't it?"

Janel wouldn't let it go. "I'm worried about Ruthanne. I hope she's all right. Do you think her husband knows?"

I said nothing.

"I honestly don't know how she can drink and take care of Jon."

"Janel, did you actually see her drinking?"

"Yes. I saw her in your kitchen, pouring something in her cup."

"And I found two empty small bottles of vodka in my garbage can," I said. "James told me to stay out of it."

"So did Rich!"

"Well," I sighed, "we should try to set a good example."

At 10:30 that night the phone rang again and I heard Ruthanne's voice. "Ava, you are my best friend in the world." She was slurring her words.

"Ruthanne, it's late. Is everything all right?"

"No. Nothing's all right. Tonight Walter went out of town again. This is so hard for me. It seems like he's never home anymore." She sounded sad and very drunk.

"Ruthanne, is Jon asleep?"

"Yes, he's asleep."

"Why don't you get a good night's sleep and I'll talk to you about this in the morning?"

She started to cry. "You're so nice," she said. "I need to be more like you."

"Everything will be all right, Ruthanne. Just get some sleep, okay?"

"Okay."

James turned over in bed. "Who was that?"

"Ruthanne."

"She probably won't remember she called you."

"I know."

"She sounds like a very unhappy woman, and drinking is making it worse. I hope her husband knows."

"Her husband travels all the time."

"Ruthanne's a big girl, Ava. Hopefully she'll figure this out sooner rather than later."

I didn't sleep much that night thinking about Ruthanne and her drinking. I also thought about Taylor and the man I saw her with, and Taylor's husband, Brandon, who was having an affair with Merrick, and about Sonja with a very ill child who was facing life-threatening surgery. So many dilemmas!

The next morning an attractively dressed Merrick arrived unexpectedly on my doorstep with Bobby in his stroller. "Could you join us for a walk to the park?" I wondered if she wanted to talk about my seeing her and Brandon at the restaurant.

I took a deep breath. "Sure. Give me a few minutes to get Jill's stroller."

Merrick started to tell me not about my seeing her and Brandon together but about her husband's side of the family. "He has two brothers who are homosexual, and my husband is deathly afraid that Bobby is going to turn out that way, too."

"I don't think you need to worry about that, Merrick. You'll always be his mother and you will love him unconditionally, right?"

"I know, I know. But Robert thinks we need to do everything possible to make sure Bobby is okay."

"'Okay'?" I couldn't believe we were having this conversation. Any child is 'okay,' no matter what their sexual orientation. I had no words for her.

We walked to the oak tree. "I really shouldn't worry about this," Merrick confided. "Look at Sonja and her troubles with Kenny's health."

"Merrick, you're a first-time mom. You're worried about everything. I know I was with my first child."

"I guess I am worrying for no reason," she said, twisting her diamond ring around and around on her finger.

"What brought this up in the first place?" I asked.

"Last night my husband got in an argument with one of his brothers. He told him he doesn't believe in his lifestyle and doesn't want to talk to him anymore."

"Oh, no."

"So my husband cut him off, but before that his brother said, 'What if Bobby is just like me? What will you do then?'" She was almost in tears. "My husband said he would disown him." Her voice shook. "He said he would walk away from his own son!"

We were almost back to my house when she turned to me. "Okay, now I need to tell you about Brandon and me."

Oh, no, she's going to talk about when I saw the two of them together. I took a deep breath and looked right at her. "No, you don't need to." The less I knew the better.

Merrick just looked at me and kept on talking. "I first met Brandon when he was on a business trip out here, looking for a house to buy before he and his wife moved out from New Jersey. He found the house that Robert and I were selling. You know I manage properties for my parents, and since my parents are very sick I've taken over the management of all of them."

I had nothing to say, so I just listened.

"I don't know how it happened or why I even let it happen, but before the house closed, Brandon and I were involved. I knew it was wrong and so did he. I feel terrible about it."

"Oh," I said. I didn't know what else to say.

"I've never done anything like this before. That night you saw us I was prepared to tell him I was going to stop seeing him. It was getting too dangerous to continue."

I just looked at her. I couldn't believe she was telling me all this.

"Taylor has no idea." She looked right at me. "I know you won't tell anyone, Ava."

James had told me not to get involved, and here was Merrick telling me all about her affair with Brandon and about her husband's brothers. She had no idea that Janel was also at the restaurant that night, and that I had spoken about it to both James and to Janel. That wasn't staying out of it at all! What a mess.

The next baby group was at Janel's and we were all there, waiting for Sonja. Kenny's surgery was scheduled for the following week, and we were talking about meals we would make for them. Sonja was supposed to stop by late, after Kenny had his blood work done, but instead we got a phone call. Sonja was crying. Kenny was in the hospital having emergency surgery!

Janel asked if there was anything she needed from her home.

"That's really sweet of you," Sonja said, "but I had the maid bring me some things."

"We will keep your family in our prayers," Janel said. "And Sonja, if you need anything, don't hesitate to call. We're here to help."

After baby group I rushed home and waited for James so we could drive over to the hospital and be with Janel. We located the waiting room for the pediatric cardiac ward and found Mitch and Sonja sitting quietly, holding hands.

Sonja hugged us. "The surgery is taking much longer than expected."

We sat with them, and finally after an hour the doctor walked in and took them aside.

Later all I remembered was Mitch and Sonja weeping. She looked white as a sheet. Janel and I hugged each other and started to cry. We had no idea what had been said, whether Kenny was alive or what; we just knew it must be very bad news. We waited a few more minutes, and then Mitch and Sonja came back to the waiting room and told us.

Kenny had died during surgery.

The pain on Sonja and Mitch's faces was unbearable. Janel and I went out to the car and cried.

When I walked in the house James tried to console me. I tiptoed into Jill's bedroom and looked down at her sleeping peacefully in her crib. Sonja and Mitch would never again be able to hold their beautiful son. James walked up behind me. "It's going to be tough for them," he whispered. I hugged him and cried.

The following morning Sonja called and asked if I could come over. I worried that bringing Jill with me would be hard for them, but I had no choice.

A very sad maid answered Sonja's door. Sonja looked even worse, her face appearing much older than usual and quite drawn. Mitch scooped Jill out of my arms and held her, sobbing, while Sonja and I hugged each other.

"We'll have a funeral service in two days," she said when we went into the kitchen. "It will be small, and I hope the baby group will come and bring all their children."

"I'll let everyone know," I said. We held each other's hands for a long time, saying nothing. When I heard Jill crying in the other room, Mitch stepped in and asked if he could give her a bottle. I took one out of the diaper bag and handed it to him. Sonja walked over to Jill and sat very close to him. Jill calmed down immediately.

"This means I won't be part of the baby group now," Sonja said through her tears.

"No it doesn't, Sonja. You're always welcome to come."

"Kenny was born with genetic defects," Mitch said. He didn't say anything else about that, but he did add, "If we adopt later, we won't have to worry about this heartache again."

Sonja just sobbed. "I would give all our money for Kenny to be back in our arms. How could this happen?"

Mitch spent the whole time I was there holding Jill in his arms. I knew instinctively that was helping him.

Then the doorbell rang, and our parish priest was there to help make preparations for the funeral. I decided it was time for Jill and me to leave. As I walked to the door, Mitch whispered, "Please include Sonja in the baby group. She talks nonstop about how nice you all are."

The day of the funeral, Ruthanne called. "Ava, I just can't bring myself to go the funeral. Do you think Sonja will notice I'm not there?"

I didn't reply. Later, when James and Jill and I arrived at the church, we sat next to Janel and Rich and their Mandy. Mitch and Sonja held themselves together the best they could all through the service, and afterward I watched their family members hug each other. The small white coffin in front of the altar had a beautiful bouquet of baby's breath and light blue flowers on top.

The service was short. Very few of us had dry eyes.

James and I planned to stop in at Sonja and Mitch's home for just a few minutes after the funeral; when we got there it looked as if they had been expecting a lot of people and only a handful had arrived. So we stayed.

I saw a trim-looking Taylor and her husband, Brandon, walk in the front door, with Merrick and Robert right behind them. I felt very nervous about that. Janel and Rich arrived shortly afterward. Merrick and Taylor introduced their husbands to Sonja and Mitch, and then to one another. It was very awkward. Merrick extended her hand to Brandon and then quickly dropped it. She kept her eyes down and moved Robert away from Brandon and Taylor.

I watched Merrick tense up. *How can she stand there with her husband and her lover not only in the same room, but talking to each other?*

Taylor kept following the women in the baby group with her eyes, and I could see Brandon's uneasiness; he kept looking at Merrick across the room. Was I the only one who could see this?

Taylor walked over to Sonja and asked her if she would come to baby group the following week. Sonja replied that she would, providing she could get out of bed. When I heard that, I moved close to her.

"Sonja, I can come to get you. We really want you to come."

James was talking to Rich and Robert. I was talking to Taylor and Janel and Sonja. Brandon and Merrick were walking by themselves down the long hallway filled with photos of Sonja and

Mitch. No one seemed to notice they were gone, and then Robert said, "Where's Merrick?"

"Maybe she's in the kitchen," I said quickly.

When the two of them finally reentered the living room, people stared at them. Merrick's face was flushed. "Sonja, those photos of your life are incredible," she said. "It looks as though you've traveled the world and then some."

Sonja started to cry. Mitch put his arm around her and walked her into the back yard to get some fresh air. Standing in the living room were Robert and Merrick, Janel and Rich, and Brandon and Taylor. We were all making small talk when Janel said suddenly, "Where are Samantha and Ruthanne?"

"Ruthanne couldn't make it," I said. "And I have no idea where Samantha is."

Park Day

Months passed. Today we were taking the toddlers to another park downtown that had a huge children's play area. I brought coffee and snacks for everyone and placed it all on the quilt at the edge of the playground. Sonja had come with me and helped me get things organized.

Janel and Mandy arrived and we hugged each other. Samantha arrived with Alice, and I noticed she was wearing very large dark sunglasses.

"How are you, Samantha?" I asked.

"Oh, silly me. I accidentally fell and hit the corner of my eye."

"What were you doing?"

There was a long pause and Janel and I looked at each other. Over the past year Samantha had had many "silly-me" accidents. I wasn't the only one who noticed.

Janel gently asked Samantha to take off her sunglasses so she could see, and Samantha put her head down. Then, very slowly, she removed her glasses.

Her eye was bloodshot, and a huge black-and-blue bruise marked one area. A gash in the corner of her eye had been closed with stitches.

"Oh, Samantha," Janel and I said at the same time. "What happened?"

Samantha started to cry, and Janel and I put our arms around her. "Someone is doing this to you, right?" Janel asked.

Samantha's head drooped like a beaten child's, and she nodded. We all just sat there for a few minutes. Oh, God, what must her life be like? What could we do to help her?

Sonja bristled. "Samantha, Mitch is a doctor. He has connections to help you with domestic violence."

Then Samantha started to talk. "Greg started hitting me when he lost his job about two years ago. He gets so angry, and I know it's my fault because the house isn't clean enough and I'm a lousy cook."

"That doesn't give him the right to beat you up," Sonja interjected. "No one has that right."

"I know, I know. It's just hard to leave, and if I did that he might do something else to me."

"Samantha," Sonja said, "you are coming with me right now to see Mitch. He will know what you need to do."

We hugged Samantha and the two of them left. "We'll be in touch," Sonja said as she walked away.

* * *

A week later, Ruthanne arrived late for baby group, and I noticed her tripping over the sidewalk trying to hang on to Jon. "I have the worst headache today," she said. "Ava, could you help me?"

I took Jill's and Jon's hands and walked them into the sandbox. Janel and Mandy followed us. "Something is wrong with Ruthanne," Janel whispered. "Do you see it?"

"I see it. Let's talk afterwards."

Merrick and Bobby arrived, and then Taylor and Megan. No one mentioned what had happened with Samantha. We gave the kids their snacks, and all the women enjoyed a cup of my coffee, but I noticed Ruthanne took out her own thermos and drank from it. Across the quilt Janel's gaze locked with mine.

The kids played for a few hours and we listened to their giggles until it was nap time. Then one by one the mothers and their children left the park. As Taylor left she said, "I'll see you for coffee this week, Ava?"

"Yes, you will. And Janel, too, if she can come?"

"Sure."

Ruthanne, Janel, and I were the last ones at the park. In just a few minutes Ruthanne had fallen sound asleep on my quilt, and Janel and I had watched Jon all morning. Finally we woke Ruthanne up and I noticed she was slurring her words. That was when I knew we had a real problem on our hands.

"Ruthanne," I said, "I'm going to drive you and Jon home today."

"Oh, no, that's not necessary."

Janel and I both tried to talk sense into her, but she refused to listen. She was walking so unsteadily I took her car keys away from her and used my cell phone to call her sister. Her sister was a psychiatrist in town, and I had her phone number. I explained the situation and she said she would be right over.

Ruthanne grew impatient while we waited and kept telling us she was fine to drive. She tried to pick Jon up but she lost her balance and fell down. I stuffed her car keys in my purse, and Ruthanne threw a punch at me. I ducked.

"Janel," I yelled, "do something! If her sister doesn't show up we'll have to call the police."

Ruthanne lunged for my purse and fell again, and then I heard a woman's voice shout from a distance. Ruthanne's sister ran toward us.

"Thanks for the call," she panted. "I came as fast as I could." She grabbed Jon, put him in the car seat in the back of her car, and then helped Ruthanne in beside him.

"Thanks for not calling the police," she said.

"I almost did," I told her. "When she tried to hit me, I almost did."

The car drove off and Janel and I stood staring after it. "I can't believe this all has happened," she said. "First Samantha and now Ruthanne."

"Ruthanne's going to have to get some help with her problem. I wonder if she will?"

"From the way her sister just zipped over her and picked her up, I'll bet her family has been trying to get help for her for a long time."

I couldn't wait to get home. I told James what had happened Ruthanne. "My God," he said, "Ava, your baby group has major problems! You know there will be backlash from this."

"Yes, I know."

"You did the right thing, honey."

"But James, that's not the worst thing that's happened. You've heard me mention Samantha? We've just found out that her husband is abusing her. You should have seen the gash on her face. She said it started when he lost his job."

"Is she getting help?"

"I think so. Sonja took her to Mitch's office for help. It's really hard to stay out of it when all you want to do is be supportive."

"Ava, it's one thing to be supportive, but under no circumstances should you and Jill be around Samantha's nut of a husband. I don't want him blaming you or the baby group and come after you or Jill. Your group needs to take precautions."

"You're right. I sure hope Samantha will be okay, that she gets into a safe place before anything else happens. And you know what else?"

"What?"

"It was really something to see Sonja jump right in and help her out."

That night Sonja called. "Ava, we placed Samantha and Alice in a safe house."

"My goodness, that was fast."

"Mitch says you have to act quickly in these situations."

"Where is Samantha's husband?"

"The police are talking to him. He admitted beating her up. Samantha will probably have to move out of the area when her husband gets out of jail. Why did we not see this before?"

"She always had a good reason for her "silly-me" accidents, as she kept calling them. And she kept covering them up or just not showing up when things really looked bad, I guess. Mitch and I would like to host a couples group to discuss this tomorrow night. Please come, and bring James and Jill. Janel and Rich and Mandy will be there, too. The other ladies don't know about it yet."

"Sonja, are you really up to this?"

"I have to get back into life sometime, Ava. Helping Samantha today made me see this more clearly."

"Okay, James and I will be there tomorrow night."

* * *

When we arrived at Sonja's house the next evening, Mitch began to talk about what the baby group as a whole should do. "Even though Samantha's husband is being dealt with, that does not mean all is well. He may connect you all with what happened yesterday. Samantha has been cautioned not to tell her husband about your baby group, and come to find out she has never told her husband about joining it."

"Will she be here in town?" I asked.

"That's hard to say. She may just disappear for a while."

I wondered if Ruthanne knew about Samantha's situation since it was Ruthanne who had brought her to the baby group in the first place. I asked Janel if we should talk to her.

"I think Ruthanne is dealing with her own problems right now," Janel said. "Maybe we should wait until someone asks questions about Samantha."

"Mitch," James asked, "how long do they keep a husband in custody when this sort of thing happens?"

"It depends."

"On what?"

"On the severity of the assaults."

On the way home I told James the baby group was turning into a nightmare.

"Just be safe," he said. "This is really a situation for Samantha."

I looked sideways at him. "What if she calls me? It's okay that I talk to her, right?"

"Sure. As long as her husband stays out of the picture."

"I hope she reaches out to Janel and Sonja, too. It has to be devastating for her to leave her husband and not know how she's going to manage financially."

That night Janel telephoned. "After you two left Sonja's house, Samantha called Sonja and Mitch. She was in tears and confused about how to proceed. Her husband was not taken into custody, and he's afraid his employer might get wind of this."

"You'd think he would be worried about how Samantha was doing, or Alice," I said sharply.

"Samantha said her husband is going to relocate with her and Alice, and if not with her, then with just Alice."

"Could he really do that? Take Alice?"

"I don't think so," Janel said. "But as long as her jerk of a husband is running around loose, she's going to have to look over her shoulder whenever she's out with Alice. Samantha also said she called her parents. They're going to come and find a new place for her."

"At least her parents are being supportive."

"Ava, the reason I called is that I got an awful message from Ruthanne. Did she leave a message on your phone?"

"I haven't checked my messages yet."

"Well, if it's anything like the one she left me, it sounded like she was drunk. She said all she did was take a little sip of something at the park, and how dare we call the police and get her sister involved."

"But we didn't call the police!"

"Maybe her sister said we did?"

I just sighed. "Ruthanne *was* drunk. Maybe she misunderstood what we said to her sister. Her sister probably told her the truth and Ruthanne just didn't hear it."

"What do we do now?"

"I don't know. Baby group is getting very complicated."

"You can say that again," she exclaimed.

"Samantha probably won't be there next week, and I doubt if Ruthanne will be there, either."

"I'm going to host it," Janel said. "I'll call the others, but I won't call Ruthanne. Let's let things simmer down with her."

"That might take a while," I said. Then I listened to Ruthanne's phone message. *"Ava, how dare you and Janel call the police! I did nothing wrong. I was perfectly fine to drive Jon home from the park. You two were trying to cause trouble and humiliate me in front of my sister."*

"Just ignore it," James said later. "She's obviously not well."

"I'm sure her family is trying to help her," I said.

"Stay out of it."

The next week Sonja called me, saying she had received the strangest phone call from Ruthanne. "It was almost eleven at night and she sounded drunk."

"I sighed. "What did she say?"

"She said no one had called about where baby group would be this week and that there was a conspiracy to kick her out."

"There is no conspiracy, Sonja. Remember that day Samantha came to the park all battered up and you took her to see Mitch and get help? That day Ruthanne came to the group drunk."

"At ten in the morning?"

"Yes. Janel and I took care of Jon, and Ruthanne fell asleep on the quilt until her sister came to drive her home. Ruthanne thinks we called the police on her, but we didn't." I didn't tell her how Ruthanne had tried to punch me when I took her car keys away.

"Ava, I told her that Janel was hosting the group this week. I had no idea about any of this. No one told me anything."

"We tried not to say anything more than what we needed to."

"So, I guess we will need to deal with Ruthanne at Janel's house tomorrow."

"I'll call Janel and warn her," I said.

No sooner had I hung up than Samantha called. "My parents are in town and I'm staying with them. I told them about the baby group and they want to meet everyone. Can they come?"

"Samantha, is it safe for you to be out and about? Do we need to worry about Greg trying to get Alice?"

"He's out of town for the next two weeks."

I hesitated. "Well, the group is meeting at Janel's house." *Was this putting everyone in danger? Should I have asked someone's permission before I mentioned the location?*

Later, I called James. "Ruthanne is the one I'd worry about, Ava. She's a loose cannon, doesn't know what's right or wrong.

She has a drinking problem, and that means you keep her sister's phone number handy in case you need it."

"Okay."

"Remember, this is just a baby group. You women are not professionals and you shouldn't try to solve anyone's mental problems."

Calm Before the Storm

I arrived at Janel's extra early. "I came to help with the coffee."

"I wonder what's in store for us today," she said cheerfully.

I was laying down the quilt when the doorbell rang; Samantha and her parents were standing on the porch. After they were introduced, Alice went into the playroom and started twirling so her dress would puff out. The other kids smiled and watched.

The mothers all sat on the quilt and Janel and I served coffee.

"Greg may get visitation with Alice," Samantha said. She admitted she was upset about it. "I took photos of all my injuries. How can this be?"

Samantha's father spoke up. "It won't be, after our lawyer gets hold of him." We all stared at him.

"I hope you're right, Dad," Samantha said.

Then Ruthanne appeared with Jon and her sister, Jane. Jane waited on the porch to be invited in, but Ruthanne walked right in as if she didn't need an invitation. Janel was surprised, but she shook Jane's extended hand and invited her to join the others.

Ruthanne stood near the quilt and let her sister do the talking. "I'm sorry if I have to be serious here for a minute," Jane began. "But for Ruthanne's sake I need to be. Ruthanne has a drinking problem. Last week we enrolled her in a program that starts at one o'clock every day. They want her to keep the good things in her life and get rid of the stress-filled things that ultimately lead to her drinking."

So, I thought, baby group was a good thing! But I did wonder if the other women thought it was a good thing for Ruthanne to be there.

Jane sat down next to Jon, where Jill and Mandy and Alice were playing, and then Ruthanne spoke. "I am very sorry for what I did at baby group last week. I've been struggling with this problem for a while. Jane told me what really happened that day at the park, and I'm embarrassed that I lost control. I want you all to know that I'm working on it."

All of us could see how difficult it was for her to say this out loud. She was lucky to have her sister's support.

Then Merrick and Taylor arrived. Bobby and Megan started to play with the other kids while Samantha introduced her parents and Ruthanne introduced her sister. When it came time to leave, Jane came up to me and spoke so quietly only I could hear. "It's taken our family some time to see Ruthanne's problem. I want to thank you for giving her a second chance. I know you could have called the police, and I'm really grateful you called me instead."

That made me feel that I had helped, even if it was just a little. It was a good feeling.

That night James told me we would be entertaining clients from Europe next Monday evening. "Some new restaurant in the city," he said.

I went to bed that night wondering if baby group things were finally going in a good direction. Or if it was the calm before the storm?

The Letter

Fall came, and the weather was changing to cool, brisk days. Baby group was meeting at my house this week, and I knew it had to be inside because it was too chilly to sit outside. James and I were entertaining business associates that night, so I was busy dusting and picking up after the older kids when the phone rang. It was James.

"Ava, we need to be right on time for dinner."

"It's all arranged," I assured him. "Gina will stay and watch Jill."

I went out to get the mail and immediately spied a letter from an attorney's office. When I opened it I was so upset I tried to call James back, but his secretary said he was in a meeting. Then the phone rang.

It was Janel, and she sounded distraught. "Ava, I just got a letter from Samantha's husband's attorney. Alice is not to be allowed in our home without Greg's supervision or his permission. Can he do this?"

"I have no idea, but I got the same letter."

"Did anyone else?"

"I don't know."

"I guess we'll find out soon enough, but I'm worried."

"You know, Janel, I think this might be a scare tactic Greg is pulling to make Samantha's life miserable."

"Huh! He's trying to scare *all* of us. And he's doing a good job. I am really upset that he knows where we all live. I thought he didn't know about the baby group."

James called 30 minutes later. I told him about the letter from Greg's attorney, and he said he'd come home for lunch and take the letter back to the office and have their attorney look at it. "There's really nothing I can comment on until I see the actual letter."

I was so upset I could not concentrate on anything. When James finally arrived he opened the letter and scanned it. "It's a scare tactic," he said. "We don't need to respond."

"We don't?"

"He probably wrote another letter to Samantha in more detail. Ava, you need to stay out of this one. And for God's sake, don't have Samantha at baby group until she clears up this matter with her husband. He's bad news, and from the looks of it he'll cause problems for all of us if either Alice or Samantha is in our home. This is not a stable person you're dealing with."

I felt terrible for Samantha, and I couldn't help wondering what kind of letter she had received from her crazy husband. Later that afternoon Sonja called. She'd received a letter from Greg's attorney stating the same thing. "Mitch said we shouldn't have

Samantha at baby group until she gets full legal custody of Alice. What a shame for her."

"Yes, but there's really nothing we can do about the situation right now. The last thing any of us need is to get in the middle of their marital dispute."

* * *

James and I were the first to be seated at our reserved table in the restaurant. Couples kept arriving until there were 10 of us around a large round table. The woman next to me was a lawyer, taking some vacation time to travel with her husband. I asked her what kind of law she practiced, and she said she was a divorce lawyer.

My interest perked up. I let her talk about herself and her family for a while before I got up the nerve to ask what I wanted to know. "Have you ever heard of a divorcing couple situation where the husband sends notices out to friends that his wife and young daughter cannot be in their homes without his permission?"

"No. I've never heard of such a thing."

"It's happening in my baby group. One of our members is trying to get away from her abusive husband."

"He sounds unreasonable," she said. I was sure she meant to say he sounded like a nut.

The dinner went on for hours, and when we left the lawyer said to me, "Good luck with your baby group situation."

On the way home I told James what she had told me. "See?" he said. "I told you the right thing. The guy is nuts."

I wondered who else had received letters from Greg's attorney.

When we arrived at home the kids were finishing up their homework and Jill was sound asleep. "Mom," Gina said, "some lady named Samantha called and said she'd see you at baby group tomorrow."

James shook his head. "You'd better call her first thing in the morning and clear this up."

"But I don't have her new phone number. She's moved to a place no one is supposed to know about."

He looked at me. "Then you'd better meet her at the door and tell her about the letter you received."

I guess I looked upset. He came over and gave me a hug. "You have to do this, honey. This guy is a nut."

It was too late to call Janel, but I did first thing in the morning when I woke up. "Samantha left a message last night saying she was coming to baby group today."

"What? She can't."

"James said to greet her at the door, tell her what has happened, and not let her in."

"I will come early," she assured me.

At 9:45, Janel was at the front door, then Merrick and Taylor arrived, and then Sonja. They had all gotten letters! We checked to see if they were identical. They were.

"How did Greg find out where we all lived?" Sonja asked. No one said a word, so it remained a mystery. The only women absent today were Ruthanne and Samantha.

The kids were playing with the toys I'd left for them, and I was in the kitchen getting the coffee when the doorbell rang. Janel jumped up to open it.

There stood Samantha with Alice. She was about to walk into the house when Janel stopped her. "Samantha, we all received letters from Greg's attorney stating that Alice cannot be in any of our homes without his permission."

Samantha was dumbfounded.

I came to the door. "Samantha, did you receive a letter, too?"

"No. What letter are you talking about?"

The women waved their letters in front of her like flags. I gave her mine, and she stood there reading it, then burst into tears. "This means I can't bring Alice inside?"

Oh, God, I felt just terrible. "I am really sorry, Samantha. According to Greg's attorney, if he finds out he could sue us."

"Wait a minute," Sonja said all of a sudden. "Let's just go to the park! The letter didn't say anything about a meeting outside our homes, like at a park, right?"

All of us looked at each other, immediately packed everything up, and walked down the street to the park. Janel stopped me near the big oak tree. "Gosh, Ava, what if Greg does something anyway?"

"I know. I'm nervous about this whole thing." I put the quilt on the grass and we put jackets on the kids to keep them warm while they played in the sandbox.

Half an hour later Ruthanne arrived with Jon and her sister, Jane. Ruthanne said nothing about getting a letter. At lunch Samantha asked where baby group would be the following week, and we all started talking about the letter.

"What if it's too cold to meet outside?" someone said.

Janel looked at us. "Could we go to another park?"

Then Samantha spoke up. "I'm going to take care of this nonsense once and for all. I'm calling the attorney handling our divorce and I'll find out what this is all about. I'll call one of you before baby group next week."

Janel and I left together. "Ruthanne never said whether she got a letter," Janel remarked. "Rich won't like Samantha coming to our house next week."

"I hope going to the park today was okay," I said. "We better figure this out before next week."

Janel frowned. "Didn't we already figure it out, and then Samantha just showed up?"

"Yes," I sighed. "It's getting too cold to meet outside. But remember, Samantha said she was going to call her lawyer and get to the bottom of this whole thing."

"Yeah." Janel's voice sounded doubtful. "I guess we'll find out soon enough."

* * *

Two days later I was getting the older kids out the door for school when the phone rang. I almost didn't answer it, but something stopped me.

"Ava, it's Samantha."

"Samantha! I can't talk now, I'm rushing out the door to take the kids to school."

"Could you meet me downtown for coffee? And bring that letter with you, okay?"

I grabbed the letter off the counter and headed for the car. Why did she want me to bring it?

I walked into the coffee shop and waved when I saw her across the room. I slid into the booth and put Jill in a highchair at the end of the table, ordered some coffee, and took a toy out of my diaper bag for her. "What's up, Samantha?"

"I have something important to tell you. I spoke with my lawyer and he talked to Greg's lawyer about that letter you all got."

"And?"

"They said they didn't send any letter to any of you."

"What?"

She shook her head. "Did you bring your copy of the letter?"

"Right here." I took it out of my purse.

"Can I take it to my lawyer? I'll give it back at the next baby group."

"Sure." I handed it to her. We both looked at it.

"It sure looks official," she said.

"Is this Greg's lawyer, Patrick Pender, Attorney at Law? If they didn't send it, then who did?"

"I have no idea. My lawyer wants to see it."

"So your lawyer doesn't see a problem if you and Alice come to baby group?"

"No. In fact he thought it was a stupid demand."

"We agree on that, right?" Samantha and I chuckled. "But now we have a mystery—who really sent that letter?"

"Where is baby group next week, Ava?"

"Janel's house. Samantha, call me as soon as you find out about this. Then I'll call everyone and let them know it's okay for you to come to baby group at our homes."

I went to the grocery store, and when I got home the phone was ringing. "Ava," Samantha said, talking very rapidly. "The letter is a fake. It's not even the correct letterhead for Greg's attorney."

"Really? What does this mean?"

"If we can figure out who sent the letters," she said in a decisive voice, "then the law firm could make problems for them trying to use their firm to make threats. That is illegal."

"Oh, wow. At least you can come to baby group now with no worries. That is really strange, though. Who would go to all this trouble, and why direct it at the baby group?"

"I wish I knew," she said.

"I think whoever sent the letters didn't want you to come to baby group! And they wanted to make more problems between you and Greg."

"But that's really strange. Greg would certainly never do anything this stupid."

Or would he? I didn't want to even think about how strange it was.

That night I had another conversation with Janel about the letters. "Rich thinks someone in the group did it."

"James thinks the same thing! I just didn't want to say it out loud. I'm going to keep my ears open in case one of the women says anything unusual."

At the next baby group I watched everyone arrive and listened closely to what they had to say. Sonja arrived first and said she had some news.

"Mitch and I are going to adopt a little girl from Korea. She's two years old. We started the process six months after Kenny died, and just this week we were accepted. We'll get her in a month and a half."

Janel and I rushed to give her big hugs. "That's great news, Sonja." Janel said. "Really great news!"

"I'm really happy for you," I added.

Sonja was smiling from ear to ear, but then she said solemnly, "Please don't tell the other women until we have her in our arms, okay? I'm not ready for anyone to tell me anything about adopting."

I looked at her in surprise. "Why would you think they would say anything but nice things?"

"Oh, Ava, women can be so catty. And they all have their own ideas about how a family should come about."

Taylor arrived with Megan; she was not in a good mood. She brushed past Janel and said, "You would think Megan would be sleeping during the night, especially since she's well over a year and a half old."

"Oh, Taylor," I said. "She will eventually."

"I don't think I'll ever get a full night's sleep, and with Brandon traveling just about every week and…" Her voice trailed off.

Merrick arrived with Bobby and she was all smiles. "Robert surprised me with a two-night trip to the coast! Just Robert and me. Just think, two nights to sleep in! I told him he didn't even need to come, he could just send me anywhere because all I was going to do was sleep."

Samantha arrived next. She got Alice settled in with the group of kids and then she started to talk about the letter. "I want to apologize for the commotion this letter has caused." She took my letter out of her diaper bag and handed it back to me. I laid it on the floor next to the quilt.

"What do you think is going on, Samantha?" Janel asked.

She shook her head. "I have no idea. My lawyer wants me to get to the bottom of it and expose whoever did this. Apparently the person stole the letterhead stationery and envelopes, and that is illegal. The lawyer thinks it's someone I know well, someone who is trying to get back at me for something. But I have no idea what I have ever done to anyone."

"You can be sure I didn't send them out," I said.

"Neither did I," said Janel.

"Nor I," Taylor added.

"It wasn't me," Sonja stated firmly. "I didn't even know who you were until the baby group started."

Samantha sighed. "It's a mystery to me. Who would want to cause trouble for me? I guess I may never find out."

An uneasy silence fell, and then she went on. "I wanted to tell you that Greg is getting some professional help with his depression and anger. He asked me to hold off on divorcing him until he gets better."

We all looked at her. Janel was the first to speak. "What are you going to do?"

"My parents want me to just walk away from him," Samantha said slowly. "Before he lost his job, he'd never done anything like this to me, and part of me wants to give him another chance. Maybe I should, for Alice's sake."

Taylor made a face. "Maybe you should see how much he actually works on himself."

"Just make sure you listen to yourself, Samantha," Janel advised. "Make sure he really is trying to fix his problem. It's not *your* problem. It's his." She stood up to get more coffee for everyone and the doorbell rang. Ruthanne and Jon came in.

Ruthanne wore tight leather pants and a loose white blouse, and huge, bright gold earrings dangled from her earlobes. Five bangles clanged on her wrist, and her shoes had 5-inch heels. Just looking at them made my feet hurt.

"Sorry we're so late today," she said. She moved to the quilt, took off her heels, and put them on top of my letter from Greg's attorney.

"Where is your sister today?" Janel asked.

"Oh, Jane had another appointment. Besides, I figure I need to get out without family sometimes. After baby group I go straight to my AA meeting. I'm feeling good."

Taylor smiled at her. "That's great, Ruthanne. Good for you."

Before we knew it, nap time came for the little ones and that meant lunch time for us. The women started to leave, and I went to fold up my quilt. Ruthanne lifted her shoes.

"What's this?" she said. She had my letter in her hand.

"Oh," I said. "That's my copy of the letter."

"What letter?"

"The one from the attorney," I said.

"What attorney?"

"Ruthanne, didn't you get a letter from Greg's attorney?"

She looked down at her feet. "Tell me about it."

Samantha explained. "A letter was apparently sent from Greg's lawyer trying to stop me and Alice from coming to baby group."

"Oh, my goodness!" Ruthanne exclaimed. I noticed that Samantha had not mentioned that the letter was not from Greg's lawyer at all; it had been faked.

Ruthanne looked up at Samantha. "Greg is really making it hard on you, isn't he? Well, you can always count on me to stand by you. Greg is a jerk." Then she mistakenly put my letter in her purse. "Ava, could you watch Jon for a minute?"

"Sure." She went to the restroom and I grabbed her purse, which she'd left wide open. I could see my letter. I caught Janel's eye and tipped my head toward Ruthanne's purse. She peeked inside and gasped. There were two letters.

"Didn't Ruthanne say she didn't receive a letter?"

"Yes."

Just then Ruthanne walked back into the room. "Ruthanne," I said, "can I have my letter back?"

She glanced down and saw that her purse was open. Quickly she took out my letter and snapped her purse shut. "I have to go now." She gave Samantha a big hug. "If there's anything I can do for you, call me anytime, day or night."

Samantha stared at her. "Just work on your own troubles right now, Ruthanne. I'll deal with mine."

When everyone left, I turned to Janel. "Did you see that? Ruthanne had my letter in her purse, and there was also another one just like it! Both looked just like ours."

"But she said she didn't get one, didn't she?"

"She sure did," I said.

"What do you think is going on? Why would she say she didn't get a letter when she obviously did?"

"I don't know. It was definitely the same as ours, but I didn't see an envelope." I thought for a moment. "Remember, Ruthanne was the one who brought Samantha into the baby group. I assumed they were good friends."

Janel shook her head. "Maybe they're not as good friends as we think they are."

The Halloween Party

"Mitch and I are having a big Halloween party," Sonja announced on the phone. "We'll all dress up and it'll be fun!" She sounded happy. What a nice change for her and her husband.

They always had big parties; they would decorate their whole house according to whatever holiday it was. That night James and I drove over to find orange lights along the roof and large pumpkins all over the front yard. A huge spider hung from the chimney, and white cobwebs were draped along the shrubbery. A Caution tape marked off the front door, along with a sign: Enter At Your Own Risk.

Just inside the front entry stood an 8-foot knight in armor, holding a sword. The pictures on the wall were askew, with cobwebs and spiders all over them. Sonja told me it had taken her a month to decorate. "Mitch always grows a huge pumpkin, and this year's is the largest ever."

A jar sat in the entryway where everyone could guess the pumpkin's weight; whoever came the closest won a prize at the end of the night. Mitch greeted us and told us an official with a massive scale had come yesterday to weigh his pumpkin. He was really proud of it.

There must have been over a hundred guests, dressed in every costume imaginable. Mitch was Dracula, and Sonja was a countess. James and I and our older kids arrived as a ghost family. Taylor came as Cinderella and her husband, Brandon, was her knight in shining armor, complete with a real helmet! Merrick and Robert dressed as a caveman and cavewoman; their son, Bobby, came as a bumblebee. Samantha arrived as a witch with a huge black hat and a broom, and little Alice was a princess. Janel and Mandy came as butterflies; Rich was a caterpillar.

The music was loud. Every so often the DJ would play the hit "Thriller," and everyone jumped onto the dance floor for the Thriller dance. Sonja and Mitch were great enthusiasts of music and could really keep time with the songs blaring in the background.

Ruthanne and her husband, Walter, arrived late in fabulous costumes as Frankenstein and his bride. Their makeup was incredible. She told me they had hired a makeup artist.

By this time the music was so loud you had to yell at someone standing right in front of you. I yelled at James to come up to the observation deck with me for some quiet. We walked down the long hallway and I pointed out Sonja's and Mitch's photographs of their adventures. At the photo of Sonja in her race car, he said "Wow." Then he stopped at the photo of the boat on the Amazon. "They sure like to travel," he said.

We reached the elevator and stepped out on the observation deck; it was much quieter, but still packed with people. All at once I spied Taylor and Brandon in a far corner; Brandon had removed his helmet and they were kissing. But when I saw his face I stopped dead in my tracks.

That wasn't Brandon! It was the man I'd seen with Taylor at the restaurant almost a year ago. I grabbed my husband's arm. "Go back downstairs with me." James looked confused, but he agreed.

Janel and Rich were on the far side of the room. When I reached Janel I leaned in close and spoke in her ear. "Taylor is up on the observation deck with that guy we saw her with at the restaurant!"

"That's really stupid of her," Janel whispered. "I assumed it was Brandon under all that armor."

"So did I."

Just then I looked up to see a smiling Taylor and her armored mystery man walking out of the hallway, hand in hand. Sonja was standing at the entrance, and she began to compliment them on their costumes.

James and I walked into the crowded back yard, and there was Ruthanne standing by the bar. Janel and Rich and Mandy were right behind us. "Oh, no," Janel whispered. "Look who's over there by the bar. I hope she's not drinking."

I watched Ruthanne for a few minutes. Sure enough, she was drinking. "Is her husband here?" Janel asked.

"Yes. I saw him earlier. Where is he now, I wonder?"

"She shrugged.

When James and I left the party, I ran into Brandon coming in the front door. The real Brandon! "I just flew in from out of town," he said. "I thought I'd surprise Taylor. Any idea where she is?"

I couldn't speak. *Oh, my God, Taylor is here with someone else who's pretending to be you! When she sees her husband she's going to have a heart attack.*

"She's going to be surprised all right," I said without thinking. I turned to Janel at the front door and Brandon wandered off in search of Taylor.

"This is going to turn out badly for Taylor," I murmured.

"I think you're right," Janel whispered.

When we got home, the phone was ringing. It was Sonja. "Ava, meet me at the coffee shop downtown after twelve o'clock Mass tomorrow. Call Janel, too." The music was so loud in the background I could barely hear her. I knew something had happened.

After church the next day I drove to the downtown coffee shop and found Sonja already seated. Then Janel walked in the door and we slid into the booth.

"Taylor's husband, Brandon, came to the party last night," Sonja began. "When Taylor saw him she turned white as a sheet of paper. She ran up and kissed him, and then she linked arms with him and hustled him out the door."

"Without saying goodbye to you or Mitch?"

Sonja ignored my question. "And…" She lowered her voice. "…Taylor did something else."

"What?" Janel and I said together.

"She left that other man, the one dressed in armor, at our party. I went up to him and asked who he was."

"Sonja," Janel said quietly. "Did you know Taylor and that man are having an affair?"

"Why didn't you tell me?" Sonja said sharply.

"I saw them together at a restaurant one night," I said. "But I didn't know if it was really what it looked like. I kept hoping I was wrong."

Sonja stared at me. "He said his name was Edward. He lives in New Jersey. And…" Her voice got very quiet. "He told me he is Megan's father."

"What?" Janel yelped. "Are you kidding? Why would he tell you that?"

"Granted, he was pretty drunk. But Mitch heard him, too. He was one of the last to leave the party."

I couldn't understand why this Edward would share such a secret with perfect strangers. "What a mess."

"Edward said he'd been here in town all week," Sonja said. "I don't know what to do."

"I'm not touching this with a ten-foot pole," Janel muttered.

"But it was Taylor who said she'd want her friends to tell her if *her* husband was having an affair, wasn't it?"

Janel and I looked at her. "I'm not that friend," I said. "I don't want to destroy a marriage."

"Keep me out of it," Janel said.

Sonja nodded. "Me, too."

In the silence that followed the three of us just sat there looking at each other. Finally I got up to leave. "This is for Taylor and Brandon, and now Edward, to figure out."

On my way home I couldn't help wondering what Taylor had gotten herself into. Why had she married Brandon in the first place if she was involved with someone else? She was a Eucharist minister at church, for heaven's sake!

Out in the back yard James was playing with the kids, kicking a ball on the grass. "Ava, how was coffee with Sonja?"

"Interesting," was all I could think of to say.

Betrayal

A few of us decided to take our kids to Gymboree. The instructor was young, soft-spoken, and cheerful, and she enthusiastically showed the kids athletic movements with colored balls. Jill, Mandy, and Alice were all giggles as they passed the ball to each other, but Bobby and Jon started to act up, even though the instructor tried hard to get them to pay attention.

Jon was a darling little 2-1/2-year-old with huge brown eyes and very long eyelashes, but his angelic face hid his tendency to bully, and he was an instigator who knew which buttons to push in the other children. Bobby was blond with blue eyes, quiet and shy. Usually he followed all his mother's directions, but this was beginning to change. Jon showed Bobby that things could be accomplished through hitting, and the two of them were quickly becoming real bullies.

On this particular day the instructor had her hands full. Bobby was pulling Mandy's ponytail while Jon was heaving the ball to hit the other kids. This went on for 10 minutes and finally the instructor sent the boys back to their mothers to calm down.

Merrick and Ruthanne were not happy about this. Both of them sent their children back to the group. When Jon's hitting resumed, Merrick yelled at him from the sidelines. Ruthanne appeared very anxious, and she wanted her child to do the right thing. But both boys started hitting the girls with a blue ball. The girls started to cry, but Bobby and Jon just laughed.

Ruthanne raced onto the floor, snatched up Jon, and shook him. "Stop it!" she yelled. "Stop it!" Her face was red and angry-looking.

The look on the instructor's face said it all. She had reached her limit and would no longer tolerate this behavior, so she ordered both parents to remove their children from class for the rest of the day. "Jon is not ready for this class at this particular time," she said to Ruthanne. Then she looked at Merrick. "Neither is your son. Neither one of them follow simple directions."

Ruthanne turned on her. "How dare you tell me my child is not ready for this class!" At that point the manager appeared and asked Ruthanne and Merrick to follow her.

"I want a refund," Merrick huffed. Ruthanne just looked embarrassed.

"I am happy to give you a refund," the manager retorted. "But you might want to wait until next week and see if your children behave."

"Your instructor is terrible," Merrick said loudly. "I won't be coming back."

Sonja, Janel, and I stood dumbfounded, unable to believe what we were seeing. I watched Merrick and Ruthanne leave with their two crying children in tow.

"Gee," Sonja said softly, "Ruthanne sure lost control."

"I hope this behavior happens in her home, too," Janel added.

I sure hope not, I thought.

I told James about it that night. "Ruthanne is the one with the drinking problem, right?" he said.

"Yes, but there's never a good reason to shake a child."

"Ava, no one wants to hear that their child is not up to par with other children. Is Ruthanne still coming to your baby group?"

"As far as I know, yes."

"Keep an eye on both of them when they're around the other kids."

I was growing increasingly uneasy about some of the women and their values; it made me wonder what was going on in their homes. *What am I doing with these women, anyway?*

The next day baby group was at my house, and I was just getting everything set up for the kids when Merrick called. "Ava, I am not coming to baby group today." I was relieved. Then she went on. "About yesterday. Bobby is a little slow. I'm having trouble teaching him his ABC's and numbers, but I just flew off the handle when he wouldn't listen to the instructor. I shouldn't have overreacted."

"Just come to baby group, Merrick. You can tell the group what you just told me." I wasn't going to make excuses for her, but maybe she needed support from the other mothers.

"I'll think about it." Then she hung up.

Janel arrived, and Mandy ran to hug Jill. They'd both worn dresses and they started to twirl around and giggle. They twirled all the way to the quilt where the toys were laid out, and Janel followed me into the kitchen. "Are Merrick and Ruthanne coming today?"

"I don't know. Merrick called earlier and said she was embarrassed."

"As she should be."

A knock sounded on the front door, which turned out to be a smiling Sonja. "Is everyone coming today?"

"Merrick might not show up," Janel volunteered. "She's embarrassed about yesterday at Gymboree."

"I talked to Mitch last night. He thinks there could be a real problem there, and he told me to keep an eye out, especially for Jon."

"Ruthanne might just have had a bad day," I suggested.

"Yes," Sonja said firmly, "but she can't take it out on Jon."

Janel joined us. "This group has major problems," I said in a whisper. "Merrick and Taylor are each fooling around; Samantha is divorcing her husband who has physically abused her; and God knows what else poor little Alice has had to see. I don't want to get involved with child protective services. When do we say enough is enough?"

Janel and Sonja looked at me in silence. "How can we walk away from a little girl who may need our help?" Sonja asked.

"You know that two-year-olds push the limits all the time," I said. "I don't know when would be the right time to get involved." The fact was we were already more involved than we wanted to be. I went to answer the doorbell.

Taylor came in, all bright eyes and smiles. Megan ran over to the kids who were playing in the family room. "Sonja, that was some party you gave last weekend," Taylor remarked. She acted as if nothing unusual had occurred, and that made me wonder.

Just then Merrick and Bobby arrived. Bobby went off to play with the other kids, and right off the bat he snatched Jill's toy out of her hand. Merrick swiftly rescued it and gave it back to her. "Bobby, no!"

When I saw Bobby fling another toy at Mandy's head, I went over, wrapped him in a hug, and tickled him to district him. Then I got down on one knee so I would be at eye level with him. "Bobby, Jill had that toy first. When she is finished playing with it, then you can play with it."

Merrick shot me a startled look. "Hey, that worked. He's not yelling or kicking."

"Yelling doesn't always accomplish discipline," I said. Maybe Merrick just needed to be shown how to handle situations.

The kids were all behaving, so I served coffee and the kids had a snack. When I returned from the kitchen, I caught Sonja staring at Taylor. "Taylor, how is your week going?"

"About as usual," she said. "Megan isn't sleeping." Taylor did look tired.

"You left the party suddenly," Sonja pursued. I wondered if she was trying to ask about Taylor's boyfriend.

Taylor's face flushed, but she ignored Sonja and went to play with the kids. I wondered if Taylor realized that we knew about her boyfriend. I spread my quilt out on the back lawn and the kids started kicking balls around the yard. We all followed them outside, and then Sonja again approached Taylor.

"That was some costume the guy in armor wore at the party!" She had an odd look on her face. What was she trying to do?

Again, Taylor pretended not to hear. I went to the kitchen and Sonja followed. I turned to her and said, "Sonja, what are you trying to do? You're going after Taylor, and I think you should leave it alone. Baby group is neither the time nor the place for this."

Sonja took a deep breath. "Ava, Taylor's boyfriend, Edward, might show up at your house today."

"What?"

"Ruthanne called me last night. She was drunk. It turns out that she and Edward got to talking at my party, and she told him about the baby group and gave him directions to your house."

"No!" I blurted. "I won't let him in." I got some milk out of the refrigerator. "Doesn't Taylor see what an awkward situation her affair puts the baby group in?"

"That's the problem," Sonja said. "Taylor is trying to stop her affair. Edward told Ruthanne that he wants Megan. He says Megan is his daughter."

I stood there in disbelief.

"And there's another thing, Ava," she added. "Ruthanne told me something about Merrick and Brandon. Are the two of them having an affair?"

My God, where had Ruthanne heard about Merrick and Brandon?

"Brandon and Taylor should divorce," Sonja said, her voice matter of fact. "Brandon should marry Merrick, and Taylor should marry Edward. Then they can all live happily ever after."

"Oh, Sonja, that isn't realistic." This whole conversation seemed surreal. These people were living life dangerously, having affairs in their own back yards. This would not turn out well.

At that moment the doorbell rang. I shot a desperate look at Sonja, who just shrugged her shoulders.

"I have a feeling something awful is going to happen today," I said. "That could be Ruthanne and Jon at the door…" I swallowed hard. "…or it could be Edward." Very slowly I opened the door and heaved a big sigh of relief when I saw Ruthanne and her son.

"Did I miss anything?" she asked. She walked past me and into the back yard as if nothing unusual had happened at Gymboree the day before. She cleared her throat. "I want you all to know I should not have yelled at Jon yesterday." She looked relieved at having apologized.

"Poor little Jon," Sonja said. I shook my head at her. Sonja was sure stirring the pot today.

Ruthanne knew she had our attention. "Walter and I took Jon out for ice cream last night after dinner."

Good, I thought. Ruthanne had told her husband what happened.

"I have been under so much stress," she continued. "And I've been extra tired because I just found out I'm pregnant!" She may have been stressed, but she had a big smile on her face.

Everyone oohed and aahed, and I just watched. Would being pregnant with a drinking problem affect her unborn child?

"My husband wants a girl this time," Ruthanne said. "And for the baby's sake, I need to make extra sure I don't drink."

I wondered about her phone call to Sonja.

We talked about Ruthanne's due date and how she was feeling and whether anyone else was thinking of having another child. We got so wrapped up in our conversation that when the doorbell rang no one paid much attention.

But what happened next was a real shock.

We were all sitting around the quilt on the grass, and the children were running around the back yard playing tag and giggling. I had a colorful tunnel set up, and Alice's head had just poked out of the opening when suddenly I saw something out of the corner of my eye.

"There's a strange man in my house!" I yelled. My heart raced and I got up to grab Jill. All of the women clutched their kids, too, and I took my cell phone out of my pants pocket and started to dial the police.

"Ava," Taylor yelled breathlessly from across the yard, "don't call anyone. I know him."

As we watched the back door slowly opened and a man stepped out. "Taylor, could you come over here and talk to me?"

Taylor held tight to Megan in her arms. "No, Edward. You were not invited here." She looked very upset.

I stood up, still holding Jill. "Please leave my house."

"No," Edward said from the doorway. "Not without talking to Taylor."

"Then you give me no choice. I'm calling the police."

"Please don't do that! Taylor, come here, just for a minute."

Then Janel spoke up. 'I'll hold onto Megan. You go ahead and talk to him."

Taylor nodded and started forward. As she passed me I said, "Taylor, please walk him out of my house."

She stepped inside and closed the door, and everyone started to whisper. "What just happened here?" Janel said quietly.

"Edward is Taylor's boyfriend," Sonja explained.

"How did he know where to find her?" someone asked.

"This is awful!" Merrick said. "No one should ever walk into someone's house uninvited."

"Especially the boyfriend of a married friend!" someone remarked.

I noticed Ruthanne was very quiet and kept her head down.

Merrick looked at everyone. "Who would be so stupid as to have an affair when you have a child at home?"

I couldn't believe she said that. *Who's calling the kettle black? You're having an affair with Taylor's husband!*

I exploded. "How does anyone have time to have an affair and care for a child and all the while profess that they're happily married?" I kept my eyes on Taylor and that man in my house. A few minutes later she walked out through the sliding door.

She looked awful. Her eyes were red and swollen and her head hung low. In her hand she held some papers, and she marched up to Ruthanne. "Okay, Ruthanne, why the hell did you tell Edward where I would be today?"

Ruthanne didn't look up.

"Edward said it was you who told him I would be here today. This ruins everything, Ruthanne. Everything! He was this close to being out of my life." She held up her thumb and forefinger separated by a small space. Her face was flushed and she was shaking. "Just now he served me with papers." She waved them at us. "He has it in his head that Megan may be his."

We all just sat there, and then Taylor went on, her voice shrill. "Don't you all think this is terrible?"

I just stared at her. *Yes, I think this is terrible. It was terribly stupid of you.*

"Why," Sonja asked, "did you even start this affair to begin with?"

Samantha chimed in. "You know, my therapist says that any betrayal is considered a form of abuse. Of course, it's not abuse if the person doesn't find out."

She had a point. I studied both Merrick and Taylor. *They have no idea what kind of betrayal each of them is involved in.* I noticed Ruthanne still kept her head down.

"Ruthanne," I said, "why did you bring him to my house?" I looked straight at her.

Then Sonja remarked, raising her voice, "Taylor, the night of my party it was as though you wanted to be caught. You just left Edward at my house to go home with Brandon. That was a mistake, Taylor. Edward told me everything."

Taylor's face flushed scarlet. "He…he was supposed to leave his helmet on all night," she said in a small voice. "That night I planned to break off this whole sordid thing."

I stood up and announced I was getting the kids a snack. When I walked into my kitchen I screamed, and the women all rushed to the sliding door to see what was wrong.

Edward stood in my kitchen, weeping. "She can't do this to me," he sobbed. "Taylor moved away from me, but she can't take my little girl away from me, too. I will fight this."

I confronted him. "Get out of my house. Now! You two can deal with this in court." I walked toward him, and there was Janel right behind me.

At the front door he turned. "Tell Taylor I won't let this matter go."

Shaking, I locked the door behind him. The kids were still in the back yard, and all the women had gathered in my family room. "You know that Ruthanne did this," Taylor started to say.

I cut her off. "No, Taylor. Ruthanne did *not* do this. *You* did. *You* will have to deal with this." I was furious. A strange man had entered my house uninvited. I went back into the kitchen to fix a treat for the kids, and everyone walked outside to the kiddie picnic table and huddled on the quilt, whispering. When I finally joined them Taylor said, "Megan and I are going now."

"Not until you tell us how this all happened," Sonja snapped.

"That's none of your business."

Sonja gasped and pointed a finger at her. "You turned my party upside down by leaving Edward for me to deal with. And then Ruthanne got involved and now Edward arrives here at Ava's house. Taylor, I think it's safe to say it is *already* our business."

I noticed that Merrick was very quiet and she kept fidgeting. All at once she grabbed Bobby and stood up. "I have an appointment." She looked at her watch. "I'm late."

"I'll walk you out," I said. Obviously she couldn't take where the conversation was leading. At the front door she whispered,

"Ava, have you told anyone else about seeing me at the restaurant with Brandon?"

I shook my head. "Merrick, what you do with your life is your business."

"Thank you, Ava. You are a good friend."

I closed the door behind her and locked it, then stood in my entryway and gave a sigh of relief. *Thank God she left before someone started to talk about Brandon.*

When I rejoined the group Taylor was saying, "You know I would never do anything to hurt Brandon."

I stared at her. Did she really think she had done no harm to her marriage? How could she be so devious? Merrick had left just in the nick of time.

Sonja must have read my mind. "Taylor, your marriage is in terrible jeopardy, and you've put it there by having an affair. Too bad you didn't think about that before you started it."

I couldn't believe my ears. I would never say something like that to anyone's face, even if it were true. Especially in front of her friends.

I looked at the women. "I don't know about you all, but I think talking about this in front of our two-year-olds is a bad idea."

Taylor covered her mouth and mumbled, "Oh, my God, the kids!"

I shrugged my shoulders. "Yes, the kids. They've been here the whole time."

Taylor whispered, "Should I talk to Megan about it?"

"For heaven's sake, Taylor," Sonja blurted. "No! She's only a child."

Then Janel said in her quiet voice, "I think what you are doing is terrible. Terrible for you, terrible for little Megan, and terrible for Brandon."

Taylor hung her head.

* * *

Later that night I was in the kitchen cleaning my tile countertop when Janel called. "Edward was Taylor's big mistake," she said. "But what if Merrick exposes her relationship with Brandon?"

"I thought of that this afternoon," I answered.

"What a chain of events, huh?"

"I wonder if Brandon and Taylor have any inkling they are cheating on each other?"

"I wonder if Merrick's husband has an inking *she* is cheating?" Janel said. "Did you tell James about today? I just told Rich, and he told me to stay out of it. Actually, Ava, he told me to leave the group."

"Janel, you and I could still get together if we decide to leave the group."

"Believe me, I've thought of that."

Later that evening I sat down next to James. "I need to tell you what happened at baby group today."

He turned to look at me. "What happened?"

"A man named Edward showed up in our house. He walked into our house while the baby group was in the back yard."

James sat straight up in his chair. *"What?"*

"Taylor knew him. He is her, um…the man she's having an affair with."

"Ava, this is *not* okay."

"There's more," I said. "He served Taylor some legal papers. He thinks Megan is his child."

"Ava, your baby group is like a soap opera!"

"I know. Merrick left early. She's the one having an affair with Taylor's husband."

James sighed. "Maybe you should leave the group before they suck you into more of their problems."

"I knew you would say that. Believe me, I've been thinking about that."

The phone rang. The clock on my wall said 10 o'clock. Who in the world?

"Ava, this is Ruthanne."

"Ruthanne! Why are you calling so late?" I looked over at James, who just rolled his eyes.

"I'm not drunk, Ava." She sounded out of breath. "I just got off the phone with Edward. Walter is out of town, and I needed to tell someone. Edward is serving all of us papers to testify against Taylor."

"Can he do that? Why is he involving us?"

James stared at me from across the room.

"This is a bad situation getting worse," Ruthanne said. "Apparently Edward has evidence that Megan is his child."

"Don't tell me anything else," I stated. "I don't want to know. Ruthanne, I am seriously thinking of leaving the baby group."

"Oh, don't do that, Ava."

"I am not going to be pushed into a situation that makes me uncomfortable." I hung up. I was so upset I went over to the couch and plopped down beside James. He hugged me.

"They're all adults," he said. "They made their own bad choices, and there's nothing you can do about it."

I went to bed that night, but I couldn't sleep. What a mess. Who in their right mind fools around and thinks they can get away with it? I thought about the whole situation a long time. I had less in common with these women than I thought.

At seven in the morning, Sonja called, really upset. "Ava, did you hear the news?"

"What news?"

"Robert left Merrick last night!"

All I could think of was my husband's words: *They made their own bad choices and there's nothing you can do about it.*

I felt sick to my stomach.

Plenty of Drama

The phone rang just after breakfast. "Sonja! What happened with Merrick and Robert?"

"Robert came home from work yesterday and told Merrick he'd fallen in love with his secretary."

My mouth fell open. "Well, that happens every day, it seems."

"That's not all, Ava. Robert's secretary is…male."

I was speechless. Then I remembered the conversation I'd had with Merrick on one of our walks months before, when she told me Robert was worried that their son would turn out to be gay because Robert's brothers were. "Sonja, how did you find this out?"

"Merrick and Bobby spent last night here. I'm watching Bobby while Merrick sees a lawyer today." She paused. "Ava, could you meet me for coffee?"

My mind still reeling, I loaded Jill into the car carrier and drove downtown to the coffee shop. Just as I arrived, I saw Sonja pull up in her car. And—oh, my God, Merrick was sitting in the front seat! What was she doing here?

She looked terrible. Her clothes were wrinkled, and her hair looked uncombed. Bobby was crying. I lifted him out of her arms. "Merrick, what's happening with you?"

"I've had better days," she blurted. I settled Bobby next to Jill in a booster seat, and she continued talking. "I drove Robert away to…to a *man*," she wailed. "How could this have happened to me? We were the perfect couple. What did I do to deserve this?"

I just stared at her. "You must feel awful, with all this crashing in on you."

"What did the lawyer say?" Sonja asked.

"The lawyer thinks I have a good case," she said slowly. "After all, Robert hid his real self from me all these years."

"What about counseling?" Sonja said.

"That won't really change anything."

"Merrick," I said, "you really should talk to someone about this. It would be good to get all this out."

"When was he going to tell you he was gay?" Sonja persisted.

"Apparently he knew inside when Bobby was born, but he didn't want to break up our family."

"What changed his mind?"

"When he started the affair with his secretary last year," Merrick sobbed. "A few weeks ago, the guy said that if Robert couldn't make up his mind to go forward with him, he was moving on."

Bobby reached out and took her hand. "Don't cry, Mommy."

I felt my heart crack. I slanted my eyes toward the kids. "Merrick, we should talk about this later, not in front of the kids." Under the table I took her hand and she gave me a wobbly smile.

That night Sonja called me. "Merrick and Bobby have gone back home. Robert decided to let them stay in the house."

"For how long?" I said.

"For now."

I was stunned by the whole thing. "It would be a terrible shock to find out your husband wasn't who you thought he was."

"Mitch sees this all the time in his practice," Sonja said. "He says sometimes the couple can work out an amicable living arrangement for the children's sake."

"I cannot imagine how I would react to something like that."

"Merrick said it's a good thing she's been working out of her home all these years. At least she can support them financially. And Robert will be supporting them, too."

"That's good, I guess." I didn't know what else to say. No matter what, everyone was going to suffer.

* * *

That Sunday the Eucharist ministers at church turned out to be both Merrick and Taylor, of all people. They both looked well put-together, and they both greeted me nicely. I wondered what their friends would think if they knew about their affairs and their marriages going haywire. Halfway through the service, James leaned over to me. "I think the priest would take away their ministry rights if he ever found out what's going on," he whispered.

After Mass I went up to say hello to them both. "Ava," Merrick said. "Where is the next baby group?"

I looked at her, speechless, until Taylor spoke up. "I'll host it," she said quickly.

"Okay," Merrick said.

I could hardly wait to get out of the church and go to lunch with James. When we got in the car he looked at me. "Did you tell everyone you'd decided to leave the baby group?"

"Not exactly. This whole thing with Merrick Shoemaker came up."

"What thing with Merrick? I thought the problems were with Ruthanne and Taylor and her boyfriend."

I shook my head. "Yes, you'd think that would be plenty of drama, wouldn't you? But just two days ago Merrick's husband told her he doesn't want to be married any longer. He's gay. He's leaving her for his male secretary!"

James was speechless. He turned his whole body toward me. "What did you just say?"

"James, I know it all sounds crazy. I couldn't make all this up if I wanted to."

"What is Merrick going to do?"

"She's seeing a lawyer. In the meantime, she's staying in their home, for Bobby's sake."

"If Robert was really worried about Bobby, he would have done things differently all along."

"Merrick said he just discovered it about himself a year ago."

"You mean he just woke up one morning and thought oh, gee, I might be homosexual?" he said in disbelief.

"James, I have no idea. All I know is that Merrick is devastated."

"Wait a minute, Ava. Isn't Merrick having an affair with Taylor's husband?"

"Yes, but—"

"No buts. Merrick must have suspected something at some level about Robert a while ago, but that's not the real dilemma. Now she has a child. That complicates it. It's what they both do at this point and in the future that will impact Bobby's life."

"I know." I started to cry.

"Ava, honey, this is not your problem. You don't want to be telling any of these women what to do or not do. Nothing you say will be right, and they might turn against you for sharing your opinion. You *are* getting out of the baby group, right?"

I nodded. "I told Ruthanne on the phone that I was thinking of leaving."

"Didn't you tell anyone else?"

"I…I thought Ruthanne would do that for me, since she's such a gossip. Janel is leaving the group, too."

James put the car in gear and we drove a few miles in silence. "These women are nothing like you," he said, his tone matter of fact. "You can't fix them."

"Yes, I know." I watched the buildings as we passed by. What was I going to tell everyone? Who was I to say I couldn't be around them because of their moral values? No one of us is perfect.

After dinner that night I worked up my courage and dialed Taylor. "I wanted to tell you I won't be coming to baby group."

"Oh, that's too bad," she said. "We'll miss you."

"No, Taylor, you don't understand. I won't be coming any more at all."

"What?" There was a long silence. "Is it something I said?"

Actually, yes it was, Taylor. Not something you said, but something you did. It's that affair you're having with Edward.

"No, it's nothing like that," I lied. "I'm just stepping out of it for now."

"Oh." She sounded surprised. "I really value our friendship, Ava. You're a really nice person."

Oh, God, this wasn't easy, and she was making it worse. "Listen, Taylor, with all these things happening in everyone's lives, I feel I can't really talk honestly about any of it, and I can't say anything to help any of you."

"So you're going to walk away from us?"

"I guess that's right."

"Would a good friend really walk away from a friend?"

Oh, God, this was hard. "You have a point. I need you all to know I don't condone anything you're doing, but you're right, I would never walk away from a friend."

I hung up the phone and went to sit by James on the sofa. "That didn't go very well."

"No, it didn't."

"Taylor says I'm walking away from good friends. She put it all on me, but what else could I have said?"

He looked at me and shook his head. "What you say is, 'I am no longer coming to baby group' and leave it at that. They don't need an explanation."

"James, women who are friends don't do things that way. But you heard me tell Taylor I don't condone any of their behavior. I bet they won't bring any more of their baggage to the baby group."

"I think you're mistaken, Ava."

"James, I feel like I made the whole thing worse."

"Possibly. But you need to tell the others before Taylor spreads it around."

So I called Sonja. Before I could explain she confided, "Mitch told me to get out of the baby group, too."

"And Janel's husband told her to leave as well," I said. "That makes three of us who are uncomfortable with what's going on."

"We could have our own play group, Ava. Just not tell the others."

"Ha! You know our town. They would find out."

She thought for a moment. "Ava, let's all go to Taylor's house on Tuesday and have an open discussion about this. See where it takes us."

"I guess the worst thing that could happen would be if they kicked us out."

I heard Sonja chuckle.

I didn't laugh. I did not find this the least bit funny.

Nightmare

I knew things were changing in the baby group, but it was not until the phone rang around 8 o'clock that night that I found out how much.

"Sonja has been in a terrible accident," Mitch said through tears.

"Oh, my God, Mitch!"

"She went horseback riding this morning, and somehow the horse was spooked and threw her off. She wasn't wearing a helmet." He started to sob. "I've told her time and time again to wear a helmet."

"Where is she now? What hospital?" James moved close to me and put his hand on my shoulder.

"St. James Hospital," Mitch said. "The surgeon did everything he could, but…she is in very bad shape."

"James and I will come right over."

James already had his car keys in his hand. "The older kids can watch Jill."

At the door to Sonja's hospital room, I hesitated. She lay perfectly still, with her eyes closed. Her head was wrapped in gauze and tubes were coming out of her everywhere. A machine wheezed next to her, doing her breathing.

Mitch looked exhausted and frightened. "The surgeon said she won't make it," he said. "And if she does make it..." His voice cracked. "...she'll be brain-dead."

I covered my face with my hands and started to cry. Mitch looked at James. "Can I talk to you for a minute?"

They went into the hallway and I walked over to Sonja and gently took her hand in mind. "Sonja," I said softly, "I'm here." Tears streamed down my face. 'You're going to be all right, I just know it."

I waited, hoping she would open her eyes. My heart pounded and I stroked her hand and kept waiting for her to react. She looked so pale! Oh, God, just a few days before I'd been sitting in a coffee shop downtown with her and Merrick. Sonja was full of vitality and opinions.

James and Mitch walked back in. They both looked grim, and I could tell both of them had been crying. I choked back more tears. Mitch approached me. "Sonja really admired you and James. And, Ava, you know we have started adoption proceedings. I have decided to go forward with it. I'll adjust my schedule and hire a nanny."

I just listened, and he went on. "Last week Sonja and I had decided to ask you and James to be Claire's godparents."

"Claire," I wept. "I love that name."

"Claire Sonja Travers," Mitch said. "I will pick her up in two weeks, and I am asking for your help when I fly to Korea."

"Anything, Mitch. Anything."

"I know I can't do this by myself."

"Mitch, Sonja is going to get better," I said. "Just wait."

He and James exchanged glances.

"What is it?" I said quickly.

Mitch looked over at Sonja, then at me. "Sonja is not going to recover. She is brain dead."

I thought I would faint. James moved over beside me. "Ava, Mitch needs you to fly to Korea with him to pick up Claire. He wants you to help him hire a nanny, a good one."

"I have a list," Mitch said. "Sonja had already looked into some of them. You'll help me choose the right person?"

I looked at him through tears. "I'll help any way I can." I hugged him and then James. "This is a nightmare," I whispered. "It's just not fair."

"No one ever said life is fair, Ava."

I looked at Mitch. "Are your parents on their way out?" I asked. "And Sonja's?"

"They're flying in as we speak. James will help me with the funeral, but I've asked him if you could fly to Korea with me. It's a very long trip. I would be honored if you would help me pick up Claire and help me get her through the flight."

The three of us stood around Sonja's hospital bed and held on to each other. "First Kenny," Mitch said, his voice breaking. "Now Sonja. How can this be happening?"

I hugged him. "We'll do whatever you need, Mitch," James said. "You can count on us."

"Ava, will you tell the other women?"

"Sure."

"Now," he said, "I must tell the doctors what I have decided." I looked confused, but James nodded. "We will leave now."

"I will call you in a few hours."

James nodded again and we walked to our car. "Mitch wanted to talk to me about taking Sonja off life support."

"Oh, my God, James."

James shook his head and hugged me close to him, resting his head on my shoulder. "I never thought I'd ever have to have that conversation with anyone."

When we arrived at home I called everyone in the baby group. Janel was first.

"What's wrong, Ava? You sound so upset."

I started to cry. "Sonja has had a terrible accident. She's in the hospital." I told her everything, and when I finished Janel was crying, too.

"Can I see her?" she asked.

"I don't think so. Mitch's family will be there very soon." I just couldn't tell her about the discussion between Mitch and James about life support; it was too personal.

That night I called everyone else. They all cried.

Around midnight the phone rang. It was Mitch. "Can I talk to James?"

"Sure. We are praying for you both."

He let out a big breath. "Ava, Sonja died a few minutes ago."

I started to cry again and handed the phone to James. "Mitch?" he asked. "Where are you? At home or the hospital?" After a pause he said, "I'll be right there."

James hugged me. "I'll probably stay the rest of the night with him." He kissed me goodbye.

My heart was breaking.

The next morning James walked into the house looking drained. "Let me sleep for a few hours, then wake me up. I'll tell you everything then."

I dropped the older kids off at school, then went over to Janel's house. We held onto each other and wept.

* * *

Mitch had picked out a white casket and had a heart made of baby's breath with one blue flower for Kenny and a single pink flower in the middle for Sonja. James and I arrived with our children and sat in the front pews. I saw Taylor and Brandon on one side of the church and Merrick and Robert and some other man on the other side. Merrick was crying. Ruthanne was just then walking through the back entrance doors, wearing the tightest black dress I had ever seen, a black hat with a sheer veil covering her face, and 5-inch stilettos.

The service was packed with family and friends and colleagues of Mitch's. He had made reservations for a luncheon afterwards at an Italian restaurant called Allegra. The bar was open and everyone was drinking a lot.

Someone asked him about the pending adoption. Both Taylor and Merrick asked if there was something they could do, and Mitch kept saying he had everything under control. I kept quiet.

Toward the end of lunch, Mitch whispered, "Make sure you and James come back to the house. And invite Janel and Rich." I couldn't help wondering what this was about.

Janel and I were standing by the door when Ruthanne came over. "This is just so sad," she said. Janel and I nodded. *What is really sad,* I thought, *is that Ruthanne is obviously drunk and she is three months pregnant.*

"Ruthanne," I ventured. "How are you getting home?"

"I'll call a cab."

"Where is your sister?" I pursued.

"Jane isn't my shadow, you know," Ruthanne snapped.

My eyebrows went up and I caught Janel's eye. Ruthanne needed to go home. Now. I walked over to the front desk and called her a cab. When I returned, Ruthanne bristled. "I am perfectly capable of doing that, Ava."

"I know that, Ruthanne."

Just then Mitch came up and whispered, "It's time."

Ruthanne was all ears. "Time for what?"

Mitch said calmly, "Time for you to go home now, Ruthanne. A cab is waiting out front."

I was surprised he had guessed the cab was for her.

All the family members who had flown in were gathered at Sonja and Mitch's house. Janel and I went into the kitchen to help make coffee. At the end of the afternoon, Mitch came over to James and me and handed me some airline tickets and an itinerary for the following week's flight to Korea.

"Ava is kind enough to accompany me to pick up Claire," he explained to Janel.

I was really going! James and Janel made arrangements about the children while I would be gone, and then Mitch introduced us to his family. His parents hugged James and me as well as Janel and Rich.

"Sonja really liked you two," Mitch's mother said. "You both have wonderful family lives. She was happy to know you."

My eyes welled up with tears and I could barely speak. The next thing I knew Sonja's mother was hugging me and crying along with me.

I thought I would never live through that afternoon.

Bad Behavior

Two days after the funeral Taylor called. "Can you come to baby group today?"

I hesitated. "I don't know. I'm getting ready for a trip."

"Where are you going?"

I stalled because I wasn't supposed to say anything about going to Korea with Mitch. "Just a business trip."

"Merrick, Ruthanne, and Samantha are coming, but I haven't heard from Janel yet."

As soon as I could, I telephoned Janel. "Are you going to baby group today?"

"I was going to call you," she said.

"Last week, you and I and Sonja were considering leaving the group, and then Sonja died. What should we do now?"

"I think we should go. Everyone is grieving."

I called Taylor back and told her I would be coming. "Bring the quilt," she said.

* * *

When I arrived at Taylor's, she had the coffee all ready. "Put the quilt over there on the floor for the kids." That was amusing, I thought, because now that our kids were walking and running all over the place, it was the moms who always gathered around the quilt.

Ruthanne arrived in a bright red miniskirt and shiny red high heels. Her tummy bulged out of her clingy blouse. "Hi, everyone!" She seemed chipper, and she was sober.

"Is your sister coming today?" Taylor asked.

"No, not today. We aren't speaking this week. She found out about the slip I made at Sonja's funeral."

We all stared at her, and then Janel arrived with Mandy. I was anxious to hear what she would have to say to the group. Merrick arrived, looking haggard. "Robert and his boyfriend have decided to move into the house with Bobby and me," she said casually.

"Really?" Taylor blurted. She looked at Merrick as if she was crazy. "What a jerk. You need to move on with your life."

"What about your situation, Taylor?" Merrick retorted.

"No boyfriend is living under my roof," Taylor said.

Merrick raised her voice. "Your situation is just as bad as mine. Agreed?"

Taylor started to cry. "I didn't ask for this, it all just happened. And now I have to figure it all out without ruining everything."

My God, here we all were listening to these women go on and on about their lives and no one was even mentioning Sonja! I stood up. "I think I'm going to leave."

Janel rose, too. "Wait for me, Ava. I'm going with you."

Samantha looked at us both. "Why are you two leaving?"

I took a deep breath and opened my mouth. "I cannot listen to you women talk about your affairs. Sonja has just died. I thought we would be talking about her memory."

"I have nowhere else to turn to except you guys," Taylor said.

Merrick shook her head. "I'm sorry my life is so offensive to you two perfect people!"

I had just about had enough when out of the corner of my eye I saw Ruthanne take a small vodka bottle from her purse. "Ruthanne," I called. "You're pregnant! You can't drink!"

Everyone looked at her, and then at me. "Look at all of you," I said. "Taylor, you're having an affair with someone who might be Megan's father. Merrick, your husband just left you for his male secretary and now you're all living together in the same house." I raised my voice. "And Ruthanne, you need to stop drinking!"

I was ready to scream. "Get help, all of you! Don't you see that your own actions are causing your problems?" Then I took Jill's hand and walked rapidly out the front door. Janel and Mandy were right behind me.

Janel hugged me. "Someone had to tell them what they are doing," she said. "I'm glad it wasn't me. Let's go for coffee."

When we were seated at the coffee shop, Janel leaned toward me. "Have you calmed down, Ava?"

"A little," I sighed. "That wasn't what I planned to say today."

"I know."

My cell phone had been ringing ever since I left baby group. "It's Ruthanne," I said. "I don't want to talk to her right now. Or to Taylor or Merrick, for that matter."

"I understand. Until they try to lead healthy lives, everything will stay upside down for them."

Janel's cell phone rang. When she answered her eyes went wide and she covered her mouth. "Oh, no. Really?" She hung up and took a deep breath. "Ruthanne is on her way to the hospital. She's miscarrying."

"Oh, my God, Janel. I feel awful, just awful about yelling at everyone today of all days."

"Should we go over to the hospital?"

"I don't know. Part of me wants to, but another part of me thinks it would be hypocritical."

"Let's go," Janel urged.

We arrived at the hospital to find Taylor, Merrick, and Samantha in the waiting room. Taylor's eyes narrowed when she saw me. Merrick turned her back on me.

I said nothing. Then I couldn't stand it any longer. "Did someone call Walter? Or her sister, Jane?"

They all shook their heads. I got out my cell phone and dialed Jane. A short time later she walked in with Walter. I couldn't stop myself from telling Jane what had happened at Taylor's house that morning and how terrible I felt.

"It's not your fault," Jane assured me. "Ruthanne hasn't stopped drinking, and that's what caused this."

Jane promised to call me later with an update, and I left with Janel. I knew Ruthanne would never forgive me, but I wondered if I would ever again see Taylor or Merrick or even Samantha.

Moral Dilemmas

I started to get myself organized for the trip to Korea, and that night after the kids were in bed I sat down to talk to James. "Remember when you told me I should leave the baby group?"

He looked at me over his glasses and lowered the newspaper. "Yes?"

"Well, today I left. Walked out. But before I did that, I told Merrick and Taylor to stop doing what they were doing." I deliberately left out what happened later to Ruthanne. I still felt terrible about what I'd said to her, even though I knew her miscarriage had nothing to do with me.

He put his paper down. "Now why did you do that?"

I looked at my hands. "I got caught up in the moment, I guess. I've been ready to say the obvious for a while now." Then I quickly changed the subject. "I've been looking for my passport for the trip to Korea."

"Mitch and I had lunch together today," James said. "He's getting the house ready for Claire. He said he's even thinking about moving to a smaller home."

"Don't they say not to make any major changes for at least a year after losing a spouse?"

"He's not. His parents are staying with him until he finds a trustworthy nanny. He's going to rely on your advice."

"Mitch gave me a list of potential candidates," I said. "Two applicants are coming for interviews after we get back from Korea."

"What else does he need?" James asked.

"The furniture had been delivered before Sonja passed away, so I'll keep the color scheme for any decorating I do. I told Mitch I would buy baby clothes with his mother and mother-in-law."

"I'm sure they would like that."

"I haven't mentioned the trip to Korea or baby Claire to anyone."

"Good," James said. "Keep it that way. Take your cues from Mitch."

Late that night I heard the phone ring. It was Ruthanne's sister, Jane.

"Ava, I'm sorry to call so late. I wanted you to know that Ruthanne did lose the baby, but something good came out of the situation. She's entered an in-house alcohol treatment program."

"That's wonderful. I hope it works," I said quietly.

Jane sighed. "We all do. Ruthanne's problem has affected the entire family. Walter has postponed any traveling so he can take care of Jon and be available for counseling."

"That's great."

Jane hesitated. "Ava, I have a favor to ask."

Oh, no…here it comes.

"At some point the counselors may want the baby group to be part of a counseling session."

"Jane, I don't think I am welcome in the group any longer after I walked out today. I told some of those women to deal with their problems and not inflict them on the baby group."

"Are you kidding?" She sounded surprised. "Ruthanne talks nonstop about you. She says she tries her hardest to follow what you suggest."

I was flabbergasted. "Really? My husband wants me to leave the group. He won't be happy to hear I'm going back."

"Think about it, Ava. I'll keep you posted about Ruthanne."

After I hung up the phone I called Janel. "I got a call from Ruthanne's sister, urging me not to leave the baby group."

"What are you going to do?"

"I honestly don't know."

"I heard from Taylor today," Janel said. "She wanted to know if you really think she is doing something wrong. She thought you were just stressed out about Sonja, and that's why you left the group."

"Seriously? Did she say anything about Edward?"

"Yes, she did. She acknowledges that she should not have started an affair with Edward while she was engaged to Brandon."

"And?"

"She says she is in love with both Brandon and Edward."

"Oh, man. What about Megan maybe being Edward's child and not Brandon's?"

"Taylor says there is no proof."

"Yet. But what about the moral dilemma?"

"I honestly don't think she's thinking about morality at all, Ava. She said she wants the baby group to stay intact."

"I doubt that's going to happen. Really, Janel, do you agree with what they're doing?"

"No, but maybe we can help them in some say."

"I thought this group would be fun for the kids," I said. "I wasn't planning on being a marriage counselor. The only reason I went to Taylor's house the last time was because of Sonja."

"I know," Janel said.

I had no idea what I was going to do about baby group. I thought I had taken care of the problem by walking out, but maybe not. I was probably going to get more phone calls, but at the moment I couldn't think about it. I had no time to worry about it before the trip to Korea.

* * *

Leaving my family was harder than I thought. How was I going to handle going half-way around the world and leaving them behind?

I cried at the gate and James hugged me. "Now don't worry, we'll all be okay." I looked up into his face. "But I don't think *I* will be okay, though."

Jill started to cry, and then I started in again. James's eyes welled up. He was the one who went on trips, not me.

Mitch looked over at us. "The plane's loading. We need to get going." I hung onto James's hand until the last minute, and then I turned and walked into the tunnel to the plane.

When it lifted off, I stared out the window and watched the buildings on the ground get smaller and smaller. When we climbed into the clouds, I put on my headset and took out my book.

We landed first in Tokyo for a three-hour layover, and then flew on to Seoul, South Korea, and landed at Gimpo airport. A taxi took us to the Lotte Hotel in the center of town. The next day we would pick up Claire at the orphanage.

At breakfast the next morning Mitch turned to me. "I need you to sign some papers in place of Sonja. I haven't told them about her death."

I looked at him in shock, very uncomfortable with the plan. "My word, Mitch, do you really think that's a good idea?"

"It was the only thing I could come up with so the adoption would not be delayed," he said.

"What happens if they find out?"

"We'll deal with it then. Hopefully by that time Claire will be safe and sound in America."

I needed to call James, so I excused myself to the ladies room. The phone rang and rang and finally he picked up. He sounded like he'd been sound asleep.

"Honey, it's me."

"Everything all right?" he said groggily.

"James, Mitch wants me to pose as Sonja and sign her name to the legal papers. Can I do this?"

"Mitch didn't mention a word about this to me."

"What do I do?"

"I guess you have no choice but to sign the papers. But make sure you date them the day before Sonja died, and make sure Mitch uses the same date. Let's hope no one notices."

"This really makes me uneasy. I don't want to be implicated in anything illegal."

"That's the best I can come up with right off the top of my head," James said. "We want Mitch to have Claire. We know he will take really good care of her. She won't want for anything."

Back at the table I told Mitch I'd talked to James about it. His eyebrows rose. "What did he say?"

"He says to use the day before Sonja died as the date when we both sign, so that technically Sonja was still alive."

"All right."

"James also asked me whether you had sent photos of you and Sonja to the adoption agency."

"I sent only a photo of me, since I'm Korean. They know that Sonja is Caucasian."

"Then let's go get Claire!"

The cab picked us up and drove down the wrong side of the road. "They drive like maniacs here," I said aloud. We were coming to a steep hill and a semi-truck was passing a car at the top. Just then I saw the car careen off into a ditch.

I screamed, and Mitch grabbed my hand. "Hang on." Before I knew it we were in the ditch, too, but we'd escaped being hit.

The driver said something in Korean, got back on the road, and drove on as if nothing had happened. I began to wonder if I would make it home alive.

The orphanage was over an hour's drive, in a poor part of town. We were escorted inside and sent to a room to wait. Mitch and I sat down and waited and waited, and then suddenly we heard a child crying on the other side of the door. Then a woman stood before us carrying a very small girl with the biggest black eyes I had ever seen.

She looked like a little angel. Her hair was jet black and straight, and she looked well fed. She stopped crying and looked at Mitch and then at me, then reached out to him. He lifted her into his arms. I took some pictures of the two of them, and then the woman said, "Let the mother have time with her."

I looked at Mitch, and he carefully put Claire in my arms. I smiled at her and rocked her as if I were her mother. The woman watched us for over an hour, and then announced it was time to sign the papers.

Mitch and I looked at each other. We signed the paperwork quickly and then we were in the taxi on our way back to the hotel. "Congratulations, Mitch," I said. "You're a new daddy!"

He smiled. And then he burst into tears. "Sonja would have loved being here." When he had collected himself, he thanked me.

In three days we could take Claire out of the country, so we had some time until the papers were finalized and Claire got a clean bill of health.

* * *

At the airport three days later we showed the clerk all the paperwork and our visas, and I held my breath. All at once the clerk said, "Wait, there is a problem."

My heart sank. Mitch had Claire in his arms, and he asked calmly, "What is the problem?"

"There is someone here to speak with you," the clerk said. The woman from the orphanage was waiting at the check-in desk.

My mind raced. I looked at Mitch. "Just do what I do," he whispered.

I bowed to the woman, and she turned to Mitch. "There is a mistake. You accidentally put the wrong date on the papers. Please sign here and have your wife sign and date right here."

Mitch signed and wrote today's date. I signed Sonja's name and dated it the same.

"Good luck and safe travels," the woman said with a smile. Then she was gone.

I sighed with relief when the plane doors closed. Mitch and I just looked at each other, saying nothing, and the airplane lifted off for America.

We took turns feeding Claire and keeping her entertained. A few hours into the trip she fell asleep. Mitch said he was too excited to sleep.

James was at the airport to meet us. We had been gone less than a week, but it seemed much longer. I ran into his arms. "Where are the kids?"

"They're all waiting for you at home."

On the drive home, Mitch and I told James about our wild taxi ride and about how signing the papers with the wrong date had backfired. At Mitch's house he took Claire in to meet her grandparents, who hugged and kissed her as if they'd known her all her short life. It was wonderful to see.

On the ride back to our house, James told me all the things that had happened while I'd been gone. I leaned back and closed my eyes, half-listening, until he said, "A man named Edward came over yesterday, looking for you."

My eyelids snapped open. "What?" I sat straight up, my heart racing. "Say that again?"

Complications

"*What did you say?* You talked to Edward?"

"I thought that would wake you up," James said as we turned a corner.

"James, tell me what happened!"

"This guy seems to think he's Megan's real father. He wants to get proof. Actually, he wants you to host the baby group so he can get a sample of Megan's DNA."

"Oh? How does he propose to get Megan's DNA?"

"He wants you to swab her mouth."

"That's crazy!"

"This man, Edward, says he's missing valuable time with his daughter, and even though he's served Taylor with papers, she is tying things up in the legal system."

"I don't want to get involved." I was adamant. "It would be wrong to do this. Let *them* figure out the whole mess. James, I don't understand why you would even consider getting involved. This is not like you."

"Edward seems like a really nice guy."

"What? I don't believe I'm hearing this! What Taylor is doing to Brandon is just plain wrong." I must be missing something here, I thought.

"Actually," James said, "I found out from Edward that he had tried to get this resolved before Megan was born."

I stared at my husband. "What about Merrick's affair with Brandon?"

James hesitated while unbuckling his seat belt.

"What if Brandon turns out to be the real father?" I continued. "What then?"

"Then Edward will walk away."

I just shook my head. When we got inside the house Gina said I had lots of messages. She handed me a list of phone calls to return. I groaned. I was so tired from the trip I decided to wait until morning, and I headed for bed.

The first thing I heard the next morning was the phone ringing. Merrick was on the other end, and she was hysterical. "Robert and his boyfriend, Paul, want to take Bobby and move out of state."

"He can't do that," I said. "What does your lawyer say?"

"Remember Robert told me we were going to work it out amicably? Well, I was stupid enough to stop legal proceedings and…dispense with my lawyer's services."

"Oh, Merrick, call the lawyer back right away."

"My God, Ava, this is just a nightmare."

I took a deep breath. I thought what Merrick was doing, having an affair, was wrong, but even someone who's made a mistake needs help at times. "I can watch Bobby today if you want to see your lawyer." It was all I could think of at the moment.

"Okay. I'll call you when I get an appointment."

No sooner had I hung up than the phone rang again. This time it was Taylor.

"Ava, did you know that salt and vinegar and club soda can get out any stain?"

I frowned. What did this have to do with anything? "No, Taylor, I didn't know that."

"I just wanted you to know that I got your quilt back in shape for the next baby group. I'll bring it."

Apparently what I'd said at the last baby group was being completely ignored. Or maybe this was some sort of peace offering. I coughed to cover my confusion. "I'll let you know about baby group, Taylor."

Merrick called me back. "The lawyer can see me at one o'clock."

"Bring Bobby over for lunch and he can nap here."

"You're a lifesaver, Ava. Thanks."

Janel called next. "What do you think about ballet class for the girls?"

Oh, what a relief, something *normal*. "When?"

"Tuesdays at ten o'clock."

"Tuesday? That's tomorrow!" But the more I thought about it, the better the idea seemed. "Okay, that sounds like a good idea and fun, too. Jill will love it. She already has a leotard and a tutu."

Everyone had telephoned me but Samantha, and she had left a message. I picked up the phone to return her call."

"I heard you were on a trip," she said. "Where did you go?"

I didn't want to explain, so I hedged. "Samantha, I'm in the middle breakfast here. I just wanted to return your call."

"Oh. Well, the organization for abusive partners is having a fundraiser. Would you be interested in going?"

"Uh…when is it?"

"In two weeks, on Friday, around six o'clock."

"I'll have to get back to you on that."

"Ava," she said hesitantly, "are you still doing baby group?"

"I'll have to let you know about that, too, Samantha. I need to think about it."

There was a long pause. "I hope you decide to stay. After all, you're the one who brought us all together. Oh, and I also wanted to tell you something else. Greg and I have decided to get a divorce."

"Oh?"

"Yes. He doesn't want to take any anger management classes. I told him it was mandatory, but apparently he doesn't care."

"What about doing it for Alice's sake?"

"Greg said he didn't think it was necessary."

I sighed. It certainly *was* necessary, in my opinion. But my opinion wasn't really relevant. "At least you're moving ahead." I hung up and took the older kids to school.

On the way home I stopped at Mitch's house to interview potential nannies. He greeted me at the door with Claire in his arms. She was all smiles and looked adorable in her little pink dress. His parents were on the living room floor with all the toys.

I told him I was ready to interview the candidates and take notes. The name at the top of Sonja's list was someone named Hilda. She was in her fifties and had worked as a nanny for three families, each for 10 years.

The doorbell rang, and there she was. She appeared to be in her late sixties. Her face looked swollen, and her wrinkles indicated she'd had a difficult life. She had a limp, and when she sat down she mentioned that her back was bothering her. Hilda was tall and overweight; her clothes looked outdated, and she smelled of talcum powder and cigarettes.

I made up my mind on the spot. This was not the nanny for little Claire. In fact, Claire took one look at the woman and clung to Mitch.

"Come here, sweetie pie," Hilda said. Her voice was hoarse.

Claire started to cry. "Hilda," Mitch asked, "do you smoke?"

"Only once in a while," she replied. I wrote down *smoker*.

"Have you letters of recommendation?"

"Oh, I left those at home. But here are some phone numbers you can call."

"Are these phone numbers for the families you have worked for?"

"Oh, no. I'd have to look those up." *No recommendation letters*, I wrote.

Mitch then said he would not be needing her services. "Just as well," she said. "I don't like little kids so much!"

When she left Mitch and I stared at each other. "She was terrible," he said finally.

"She must have been at the top of Sonja's list of rejects!"

"Let's start afresh," he said. "I think someone younger for sure."

The next candidate would arrive any minute; I hoped she would be better. Mitch answered the doorbell, and by then Claire and Jill were upstairs with the housekeeper.

This woman's name was Brittany. She was tall and slim and looked to be in her 20's. She wore slacks and tennis shoes, and her long blonde hair was pulled into a ponytail. She shook hands with both of us.

"Here are my letters of recommendation," she said cheerfully. "Feel free to call my former employers. Their children reached the age where the parents decided a nanny wasn't needed. I have a clean record, and I love children."

I wrote that down on my notepad as Mitch went to get Claire. When he returned, Brittany was on the floor with the toys and had a ball in her hand. Claire went to her immediately.

Half an hour later, Mitch thanked her for coming and said he would let her know within the week.

"I sure hope you give me a chance," Brittany said. "I'm honest and trustworthy." She shook both our hands and left.

Mitch and I smiled at each other. Brittany was definitely a contender. We agreed that I would interview a few more candidates before Mitch made up his mind.

I got home in time to start lunch for Bobby and Jill, and then Merrick arrived. She looked a mess, her blouse all untucked and her face haggard. "This is really wearing on me," she said sadly.

I hugged her. "It will work out, Merrick. I know it will."

* * *

Ballet class on Tuesday started at 10 sharp. Mandy wore a purple tutu and Jill was all in pink. The dance teacher had a total of six students, and they all followed her instructions while Janel and I and the other mothers sat on the sidelines, looking on.

After class the girls twirled over to us, all excited about dancing. One of the mothers looked at me and smiled. "Your daughter is lovely."

I smiled and thanked her.

"My name is Maria, and this is Alexis. She extended her hand and held mine longer than usual, which I thought was being a bit over-friendly. "Your little girl did a good job," she said.

Janel was looking at me oddly. "Come on, Ava, we need to leave if we're going to have lunch." In the parking lot she looked closely at me. "What was that all about?"

I must have looked blank. "What was *what* all about?"

"That woman. She kept holding on to your hand."

"Oh. I guess that was a bit strange," I said. I shrugged it off and we headed off for lunch.

* * *

When I announced it was time to go to our next ballet class, Jill came running and began dancing around the house in her tutu. We met Janel and Mandy at the class.

The teacher had the kids start in a circle and gave them each a wand with paper streamers attached. With huge smiles, the girls began to frolic, arms extended and big grins on their faces. Janel and I were watching Jill and Mandy when suddenly I felt hands grip my shoulders. I almost jumped out of my chair.

"Oh! You startled me, Maria." I edged forward to get out of her grasp. Janel, sitting next to me, nudged my leg with hers and our eyes met.

"How are you, my dear?" Maria inquired. Maria was a short woman, about 5 feet tall, wearing jeans and a nice shirt, untucked. She wore her hair in a blonde bob.

My eyebrows went up and I stared at her. "Are you talking to me?"

Janel again nudged me and I glanced at her out of the corner of my eye.

"Who else?" Maria said.

"Why, I'm fine, Maria." Was this woman coming on to me?

For the rest of the class I sat on the edge of my chair, close to Janel and as far away from Maria as I could get. Every time the girls did something cute, Maria leaned over and spoke in my ear. I nodded and smiled, but I felt really uncomfortable, and I noticed she kept one arm draped along the back of my chair.

As the class drew to a close I got up so fast I almost knocked Janel off her seat. "Your secret admirer is coming your way," she whispered. I shot her a look and quickly turned my head. Maria was face to face with me.

"Oops, sorry, I keep running into you." She smiled. "Are you okay?"

"I'm fine." It was a lie. I was rattled. Before I could get away she had her hand on my elbow.

I shook her off and couldn't get out of there fast enough. Janel followed me into the parking lot, laughing. "What is going on with you and Maria?"

"Nothing!" I blurted.

"Where did that woman come from, anyway?"

"I have no idea, but she is definitely making me uncomfortable."

Janel frowned at me. "You mean you really don't know her?"

"No," I said firmly. "I have no idea who she is. Or," I added, "where she's coming from."

Janel tactfully changed the subject. "Let's take the kids to the park today."

We drove to the park just down the street from my house, got the girls' toys out of the car, and changed them into play clothes. Then we walked into the playground and sat down on the bench under the oak tree.

"Quick, Ava, look!" Janel whispered. Someone was walking toward us. Good heavens, it was Maria and her daughter, Alexis!

"Janel, did you tell her we were coming to the park?"

"No."

Maria and Alexis made their way to the sandbox where the kids were playing. "Look, Mommy," Jill said excitedly, "it's the girl from ballet class."

Maria came over to our bench and sat down on the grass. "I just moved here and I found this park the first day I drove around the area. It's lovely!" She pointed down the street. "I live over there." She tipped her head in the direction of my house. I hadn't noticed any home near me on the market; I also hadn't seen any movers in the neighborhood.

"Where did you move from?" Janel asked.

Maria didn't answer, just watched the girl playing. I looked over at Janel.

Then Maria started talking about being married for 15 years when she discovered she was gay. She moved here to start a new life and find a new life partner. She had custody of her two children.

Finally I said I had to leave. Maria looked interested. "Where are you going?"

"I have some things to do before my older kids get home."

"I can watch Jill for you," she volunteered.

"Oh, that's nice of you," I managed. "But no thanks."

Janel stared at her. "Is your partner from this area, too?"

"Oh, I don't have a partner. Yet," she added significantly. She looked directly at me. That made me really uncomfortable.

"I have to go now," I said. Janel and Mandy left with Jill and me. By the time we got to Janel's car she was laughing out loud. "Ava, you have a girlfriend!" I swatted her arm, then looked back at the playground, and there were both Maria and Alexis playing in the sandbox! Maria kept looking at me.

"Janel, I don't want her to know where I live."

"She probably already knows where you live!"

"This is crazy."

Janel just chuckled.

The next day as I was backing my car out of the garage I noticed someone standing off to the side. It was Maria. I rolled my window down to say hello.

"Alexis and I are going to the park," she said. "Want to come?" She patted my arm where it rested on my car door. I stared at her hand on my arm. "Maria, how did you know where I lived?"

"I saw your address when you signed in at ballet class."

That's strange, I thought. I didn't recall putting down an address.

Maria waved to Jill in her car seat, and I continued to back down my driveway. When I arrived at Janel's for coffee I told her about Maria's turning up in my driveway. "She came to my house this morning and wanted us to spend time together with the girls," I said. "Pretty much like you and I do all the time," I added.

"This is different, Ava. Maria really likes you."

"Oh, come on. She knows I'm happily married with kids."

"So was she."

My mouth dropped open. Janel said she was teasing, but I wasn't having any of it. Then she changed the subject.

"What are we going to do about baby group?"

I sighed. "I think we have to go and at least get my quilt back. Maybe talk to everyone about what is going on."

"I have a thought," Janel said with a grin. "We could invite Maria to join baby group!"

I threw a stuffed giraffe at her. Then it was my turn to change the subject. "Have you heard from any of the women?"

"I heard about Samantha splitting up with her husband. It's really sad that he's just giving up."

I told Janel about interviewing nannies for little Claire. "She's just an adorable child; she'll be a good addition to the baby group."

"How about our separate play group?" Janel suggested.

"Oh, right," I said. I'd put our idea about forming a separate group out of my mind.

"What's new with Taylor and Merrick?" she asked.

I groaned. "Edward wants DNA testing to get custody of Megan, but Taylor won't do it voluntarily. He wants me to get a saliva sample."

"Why should you? I don't see why Taylor is still carrying on with Edward behind Brandon's back. She has nothing to lose if she goes to him and takes Megan, right?" Then, as if a lightbulb had gone off in her head, she added, "Unless Megan is neither Brandon's *or* Edward's child!"

I gasped. "Oh, my God. That would be some story."

"That might explain why she's so adamant about not giving Edward any DNA samples."

"You know, Janel, we're really lucky to be happily married." I exchanged a long look and a smile with her. But then she couldn't resist one last teasing remark.

"At least you *say* you're happily married," she said with a grin.

"Janel, you cut that out!"

* * *

The next baby group was at Taylor's house, and at the last minute Janel and I decided to go. Three weeks had passed, during which I wrestled with my conscience and my good sense. Part of me wanted to be a good person and offer help to a friend who needed it; part of me didn't want to get involved with the fallout from what I saw as really bad—and immoral—decisions.

Finally I gave in to the requests that I come join them, and I drove to Taylor's. When we got there she already had my quilt on the floor. "Looks like you got the stain out," I said.

"Yes, it was easy. I wish other things were easy, too."

Ruthanne looked tired when she arrived. Merrick asked her how she was doing. She stared at her feet for a long time. "It's been rough," she sighed. "I've had three straight weeks of in-house therapy. The doctors put me on a medication that makes me sick if I drink anything."

We all stared at her but said nothing, and she went on. "Since I had the miscarriage I've felt so guilty about what I did." She started to cry. "It's all my fault that I lost the baby. Walter tells me this is my time to get better and when I'm recovered we can decide whether or not to have another baby."

I patted her hand. "You will get better, Ruthanne. I know you will."

Everyone nodded, and then Merrick, who was sitting on one corner of the quilt, spoke up. "Robert and Paul are leaning toward moving away. My lawyer says he can't take Bobby, and I'm glad about that, but the problem is this: until a final decree as to who gets custody what percentage of the time, I'll end up having to travel wherever Robert settles for visitation."

I shook my head. "I hope you get full custody."

She looked at me with a half smile. "I sure hope so."

Then Taylor said something that shocked all of us. "Edward has served me papers requiring DNA tests for me and Megan." She looked very upset, and her hands were clasped tight together in her lap. "You...you all will find out sooner rather than later."

Find out? Find out what?

But she clammed up. I encouraged her to go on. "What will we find out?"

She got up off the blanket and looked over at the kids playing in the toy room. Then she leaned toward us and whispered, "Neither Brandon nor Edward is Megan's father."

Janel's mouth dropped open. "How could that be?"

Taylor just shook her head. "I was stupid," she blurted. "Just stupid. I was careless with protection, and look what happened. Now I'm going to hurt both Edward and Brandon, and I really love them both."

"What about the real father?" I asked. "Will you tell him?"

Taylor coughed. "I guess it's going to come out sooner or later." She didn't tell us who Megan's father really was, and I didn't press her, and neither did anyone else. But I could tell by the looks on everyone's faces they were all wondering. I felt sorry for Taylor; she was going through her own personal hell.

I had to admit to myself that some of these women were doing things that made me uncomfortable. I really disapproved, and I didn't want to be hypocritical and just accept everything as if such behavior was okay with me.

Janel was quiet. She and I were the only ones who weren't in the middle of a crisis, and when our eyes met across the quilt she briefly shook her head. I understood.

After baby group, Janel asked me to bring Jill and have lunch with her and Mandy. When we got to her house, there was Maria's car sitting in her driveway!

Janel pulled in beside her and made small talk while I got Jill out of the car. By that time both Maria and Alexis were standing next to Janel. Maria rushed up to me with a smile. "How are you doing, Ava?"

"I'm good." I looked to Janel for a sign.

"We're busy right now," Janel said. "What can I do for you?"

"I brought lunch already made for us," Maria announced. She and Alexis started walking to Janel's front door.

I cleared my throat. "How did you know we would be here today, Maria?"

"I took a guess. You have a great place here, Janel!"

By that time she had come inside with us. My eyes met Janel's and I pointed to the play area in the living room. "Let the girls play over there."

Maria went with the kids, and I went into the kitchen with Janel. "This is weird," I whispered.

"Tell me about it," Janel whispered back. "How did she find out where I live?"

"The same way she found out where *I* live, I guess."

We went into the living room and Janel took the kiddie picnic table out and we all sat down on the carpet to eat our sandwiches and fruit. Maria sat very close to me, and every time she laughed she would touch my leg.

I edged closer to Janel. When the kids finished lunch, I stood up and announced that I had to get Jill home for her nap. Maria got up to leave, too.

"See you guys at ballet class, right?"

As we were leaving, Janel stopped me. "Ava, wait a minute." I waved goodbye to Maria and closed the front door.

"What was that all about, Janel?"

"I don't know, but this is getting creepy. I did not call Maria, and I did not tell her where I lived."

"Me, either."

"What are you going to do about her?"

"Well, as long as she keeps her distance..." My voice trailed off.

"Ava, you have to talk to her."

"What do I say?"

"For starters you tell her you're not interested in her the way she is interested in you."

I thought for a minute. "Do you really think she likes me in that way? Or do you think she just wants friends?"

"She's acting like she wants you to be more than a friend, Ava. Notice how she keeps touching you any chance she gets?"

"Yes, I notice!" My mind raced. "What should I do?"

"Next ballet class, just tell her you're not interested," Janel said. "Make it clear to her."

"Janel, I never thought I'd have such a discussion with anyone."

She smiled. "Uncharted territory, huh?"

Fifteen minutes later I stepped outside to drive home and there was Maria, waiting in her car. She waved me over.

"Janel," I whispered, "come with me."

"Okay, okay."

I took Jill's hand in mind and walked over to Maria's car. Janel was right behind me with Mandy.

Maria smiled at me. "I know you think I am overwhelming you with kindness, Ava, but there is just something great about you."

"Stop right there," I blurted. "I am not gay, Maria." *There, I'd said it out loud.*

"I didn't think I was, either."

That was not the response I wanted to hear. "Look," I said firmly. "I am not going to change. I am happily married with three children, and I will not—I repeat—will *not* change."

Maria just smiled. "I'll see you at ballet class."

She drove off and Janel and I stared at each other in disbelief. "She thinks you're going to change," Janel said.

"Well, I'm not!" I was really upset. "I need to change ballet class day, Janel. Let's look into Fridays, okay?"

I drove off wondering how I would tell James about this. *Oh, by the way, a woman at ballet class who's gay thinks I am gay, too!* When I got home I went straight to the phone, called ballet class, and switched to Fridays.

Uncomfortable Chaos

That night when the dinner dishes were neatly put away and the kids all tucked in bed, I sat down next to James and gave him a kiss and a hug. Then I put my head on his shoulder.

He leaned forward to look at me. "What's wrong?"

I took a big breath. "There's this woman at Jill's ballet class who is gay."

He just looked at me. "So?"

"She thinks I'm gay, too."

"What? What makes you think that, Ava?"

I told him about the last few weeks and what Maria had said today.

"Is she part of the baby group, too?"

"No."

He shook his head and chuckled. "Gosh, Ava, that is really odd. It sort of came out of left field."

"I wish it *was* funny," I said. "But it's not. I changed ballet class to another day to avoid her. At first I ignored her, but somehow she found out where we live and also where baby group is meeting."

He frowned. "She knows where we live?"

"Yes. James, she lives down the street from the park."

"Just mind your own business, Ava. And pray that she will mind hers. If she doesn't, then we'll have to do something about it."

That night I had the strangest dream. I was in a boat, alone, in a large body of water, rowing and rowing to get some place, and all of a sudden I saw my family in a boat some distance ahead of me. I looked behind me and there was Maria in a speedboat, rushing toward me. I tried frantically to row away from her, toward my family.

I woke up with my heart racing. *I have to tell Maria to stay away from me.* I called Janel, who told me that she had also changed ballet class to Fridays. Then she went on to say, "About the baby group. Rich wants me to leave it. He says it's terrible what those women are doing to their spouses."

"I know. I feel the same way, but I can't decide what to do. I can't just walk away when they need help."

"Let's you and me meet on Wednesdays at another park, just the two of us, okay? At the park downtown."

"Sounds good. Should we tell everyone what we've decided?"

"No. Whoever is hosting baby group can tell the others."

The minute I hung up the phone, it rang again. It was Taylor. "Ava, I just wanted to let you know I'm hosting baby group this week."

I cleared my throat. "Taylor, I've decided not to attend the baby group any longer. I'm very uncomfortable with the chaos in all of your lives. To be honest, it's stressing me out."

Taylor exploded. "How dare you say this to me? You think you're too good for me, huh?" She went on and on about how the group was turning against her and it was all my fault.

"Taylor, no one is turning against you. But it is true that I don't condone the way you are all conducting your lives. You're having an affair with Edward, and I don't agree with that behavior."

"You're making fun of my life!" she blurted.

"Oh, Taylor, I'm not making fun," I said quietly. "I'm really sorry you're going through this, but you are part of the problem, too."

"Well!" she shouted. "Don't you ever call me again!" She hung up.

I stood by the phone for a few minutes, waiting for the other shoe to drop. When the phone rang I picked it up. It was the pastor from my church.

"Ava, I just received a distressing call from Taylor Carter. Do you think I could help the two of you save your friendship?"

"Father, what did Taylor tell you?"

"She said you were going through a terrible time with your husband and you are shutting people out of your life."

"What?" I gasped. "Taylor didn't tell you what was going on with her, did she?"

"No. Only that you and James were having marital problems."

181

"Father, that is the furthest thing from the truth." My mind raced. If I told him what was going on with Taylor, he would faint! To make matters worse, Taylor was a Eucharist minister.

"Father, I will call you back about this." I hung up and immediately called Janel. "Could you meet me for lunch at that restaurant by the church?"

"Sure." Before she hung up, she added, "Father Damien telephoned me earlier. He thinks Rich and I are having problems."

I laughed out loud. "What did you tell him?"

"I didn't tell him anything. I told him I would get back to him."

"Father Damien called me, too. He thinks the same thing about James and me." I didn't tell her about my phone conversation with Taylor.

I was very upset by this chain of events, and I hoped that Janel could suggest what we should tell Father Damien.

* * *

The restaurant was packed when I arrived. The red-headed waitress brought us menus, and then I got a shock. There was Father Damien! Father is young and very handsome, with blond hair and blue eyes, and he was standing at the entrance looking for someone. He saw Janel and me and walked over to our table.

"I hope you can open your hearts to communicate with Taylor," he said. "Friendships come once in a lifetime; it would be a shame to let this one pass you both by."

Janel and I stared at each other in disbelief.

Then Father Damien laid his hand on my shoulder. "Please call me and we can talk. The same goes for you, Janel." I opened my mouth to say something, and just then I saw a beautifully dressed Taylor walk into the restaurant! What was going on?

Taylor walked toward Father Damien. "Hello, Taylor. I have a table right over there." He pointed across the room. Taylor didn't say a word, just walked away.

"Father," I said, beckoning him closer. "Nothing is wrong between James and me."

"Or with Rich and me," Janel added.

Father Damien looked confused. "It's Taylor you need to talk to, Father," Janel said.

The priest looked across the room and cleared his throat. "Have a nice lunch. I'll be in touch."

Janel and I stared at each other across the table. What were the odds of meeting up at the same restaurant as Taylor and Father Damien? "Janel," I said. "You know I've been feeling uncomfortable with baby group, right?"

She nodded and stirred her coffee.

"This morning," I said quietly, "Taylor called, and I told her I wasn't going to continue with the group. She got really upset and hung up on me."

"So," Janel said, "Taylor was upset and she went to Father Damien telling tales?"

"Yes," I said. "To save face, I guess, and to hide her own guilt, Taylor told Father a lie about both our marriages."

Just then I saw Taylor race out of the restaurant, leaving Father Damien alone at his table. He rose slowly and approached us. "Taylor just confessed what is going on in her life. She felt she had to lie to me about your lives to cover up." He cleared his throat. "By the way, I hope you will keep in touch with her. She needs good people in her life."

I looked at Janel, who was staring at Father Damien. I finally spoke up. "The baby group where we see Taylor is riddled with things Janel and I don't agree with morally. It's hard to be around."

When Father Damien left, Janel looked over at me. "This has been quite a lunch!"

I shook my head and sighed. "I'm not going back to baby group now, after leaving it twice. "Father has no idea what is going on with those women, especially Merrick and Taylor."

When the girls finished eating, Janel said, "Let's take them to the park."

"Sure. You know, this is all so complicated!"

"I know," she said quietly.

"I'm sure by now the entire baby group knows what has happened."

"No doubt."

"I can't believe Taylor tried to use us to cover up her own problem."

"No doubt she is telling the whole group lies about us," Janel said with a frown.

"I tried to listen to Taylor. I even tried to help her. But then I asked myself who was I to judge?"

"Yes, I know," Janel said.

"Now," I said sadly, "it looks as if *I* was the one who did something wrong."

Telling the Truth

Friday came, and it was time for ballet class. Janel and I sat down and watched all the students form a circle with the teacher, and suddenly she nudged me. "Look over there by the door."

There was Maria, arguing with the lady at the desk. Little Alexis was all dressed up in her tutu. "Are you thinking what I am?" I whispered. "How did she find out we had changed days?"

Janel shrugged. "I don't think she will get into this class."

Maria glanced at me and nodded. I looked away, took a deep breath, and watched Jill twirling in her ballet costume. Then I felt someone sit down next to me.

Maria looked upset. "They can't get Alexis into this class." She leaned closer. "Why did you guys change ballet days?"

"I had a time conflict on Wednesdays," I said. Janel just stared at her and said nothing.

"Alexis can't get into this class because it's full," Maria said again. I was relieved. Then Alexis was pulling at Maria to let her go dance with the other girls. Instead, Maria stood up. "I hope I'll see you next week."

Oh, God," Janel whispered. "Could she really get into this class next week?"

At home, phone messages were waiting from Samantha and Taylor. James had said to cut the cord from the baby group, but I couldn't decide what to do. I didn't call either of them back.

Later that evening, Father Damien called asking a favor. Would I keep in touch with Taylor? He knew that I was aware of what was going on in her life, and she needed a friend. I said I would think about it. Father Damien had no idea what was going on with the women at baby group. Could I really pull away from Taylor and the others?

The next morning Taylor called again. "Could you come for coffee this morning?"

I wanted to refuse. Taylor sensed my hesitation and quickly added, "I have something to tell you."

I sighed. "Sure. I'll come."

When I arrived, Taylor and Megan were making cookies. Taylor told the girls they could play at the kiddie table in the family room, and when they were settled, we sat in her living room.

"Ava, I have something to tell you. I just found out Brandon is having an affair."

I said nothing for a long minute. "How did you find out?" I finally asked.

"I looked on his cell phone."

"And?"

"It's Merrick! Her number appears hundreds of times."

I took a deep breath. "Taylor, what about Edward?"

"What *about* Edward," she blurted.

"Isn't he your boyfriend? Aren't you cheating on Brandon?"

"Well, yes, but this is different. Brandon is having an affair with a friend of mine!"

"You are having an affair with Edward," I reminded her. "How is that different from Brandon's having an affair with someone?"

She had no answer. I took another big breath and went on. "This is why I have been uncomfortable with you lately, Taylor. You think this behavior is perfectly acceptable, and it's not."

"Brandon might leave me."

"Shouldn't you have thought about that before you started up with Edward?"

She started to cry. "What should I do?"

"I think you and Brandon need to talk honestly with each other. Maybe get counseling to see if you can work things out."

"What do I do about Merrick?"

"I don't know, Taylor, I really don't. Talk to Brandon. You two need to decide how to repair your marriage."

She started crying again. "Ava? Ava, th-there is s-something else, too."

Oh, God, what could be worse than all this?

"What if Megan's real father doesn't want her?"

I looked at her in confusion. That seemed the least of her problems at this point.

Her head drooped and she wouldn't meet my eyes. "Brandon loves her. Edward loves her. But," she whispered, "neither one of them is Megan's father."

I waited. I already knew that from what she'd said before in baby group, about being careless with protection. And then she dropped a bombshell. "Megan's father is…is F-Father Damien."

"*What?* What did you say? Are you saying that Father Damien is Megan's…?"

Her face crumpled and she nodded.

I stared at her for a long minute. "Taylor, don't tell me anything else. You need professional help. This news will destroy the parish. It will destroy *him*." I got up to leave.

"Ava, wait. You won't tell anyone will you?"

I was horrified that she had confided such shocking news, and I shook my head. "No, I won't tell anyone."

I left Taylor's house and drove home. James could tell something was wrong. When I told him about Father Damien he said, "This is a joke, right? How do you know she's not lying? Maybe she just wants to spread a terrible rumor?"

"But what if it's true? Father Damien is our priest!"

But maybe James was right and Taylor *was* lying. The phone started ringing. It was Janel. "Ava, I have to come over and talk to you. Now. Tonight."

I was setting the table for dinner when I heard her knock at the front door. "Rich is out of town," she said, "but I had to talk to someone."

"What on earth is wrong?"

"Did you know that Father Damien is Megan's father?"

I stared at her. "How did you hear this?"

"Taylor called today and told me. I am just sick."

I thought for a moment. "Do you really believe this? That Father Damien has led a secret life while preaching fidelity to his parishioners? Taylor told me the same thing this morning, but now it seems odd, don't you think? I'm not sure I believe it."

"Something must have happened," Janel said.

"Yes. She found out that Brandon is having an affair with Merrick."

"Ha! What's sauce for the goose…"

"There's not much we can do," I said. "But really, none of this is proven. And both of us know that Taylor has emotional problems. Maybe she's making it up?"

"If it is true, I won't be attending St. Anthony's any longer, not while Father Damien is there. I'm going to confront him tomorrow."

"Janel, it's really none of our business. You have no reason to confront him. It's his personal life, and if it is true, he certainly knows he is doing wrong. Besides, it's only Taylor's word, and she is obviously unbalanced."

"You're right." She left abruptly, but I couldn't help wondering what she would do.

I was beginning to wonder who to believe.

Unbelievable

My little town of Easthaven, Indiana, was turning into a community where one unbelievable thing after another was happening. I kept asking myself if other towns were like this, if other women in groups like my baby group were like this. I was finding out way more than I wanted to know about people and their private lives. Not only that, women were telling me things that would be devastating to *other* people in the community if they were known.

I often wondered why I didn't just walk away. It had dawned on me that maybe what Taylor had told Janel and me wasn't true, so one morning I telephoned Janel.

"What if Taylor is making all this up? We have only her word that Father Damien is involved with her. Maybe none of it is true."

"Let's just ask him," she said. "He's a priest. He hears all sorts of things."

"We can't do that! I want to stay out of it." But as I said those words I realized I was up to my eyeballs in Taylor's problem because she had confided in me. I knew too much to pretend it didn't matter, because it did!

"I'll bet anything we're not the only ones Taylor has confided in," Janel said. "I think we should wait and see what happens."

So that is exactly what we decided to do—nothing. And then Sunday came.

James and I attended church in the morning. As we walked in, Janel and Rich waved us over, and I saw Mitch and little Claire in the front pew with their new nanny, Brittany. Merrick and Bobby were behind them, and Samantha and her daughter were sitting on the far side. Father Damien was nowhere in sight.

When it was time for the sermon, a different priest introduced himself and said he was the new pastor at St. Anthony's. *The new pastor? Where was Father Damien? Had something happened to him? Had he left St. Anthony's?* Oh, my God, had Taylor been telling the truth? I looked around for her, but she wasn't at the service.

After the service, James and I went to the church hall to meet the new pastor. Janel came up to us. "This is odd," she whispered. "Could what Taylor said be true?"

I shrugged. And then Samantha walked up. "I heard what happened," she said.

Janel looked at her with widened eyes. "*What* has happened?"

"I heard that Father Damien has a family over in Ireland. He's been supporting them with parish funds."

"How do you know this?" I asked.

"The church secretary. Someone called the church to file a complaint against Father Damien. It was a woman, and she said Father Damien was the father of her child."

"Samantha, who told you this?"

"The church secretary," she said firmly.

Janel and I stared at each other. Apparently Taylor had been telling the truth. James was frowning, and the next thing I knew he was walking over to talk to the new priest. I tagged along to listen, but all I heard was the priest saying, "There will be an investigation. I cannot comment any further."

That wasn't enough for James. "This is my parish," he said. "Are you saying our priest has a family? When are you going to talk about this situation so we can ask questions about it?"

"There will be full disclosure at a church meeting this week."

The after-church crowd buzzed, and my mind was reeling. "We don't really know for sure if Taylor is involved," I murmured to Janel.

Her eyebrows went up. "Chances are it's true, don't you think? Otherwise, why did Father Damien leave?"

I had questions, too, but I decided to wait for the church meeting for answers. Until then, it was all hearsay.

James and I drove home without talking. To calm my tumbling thoughts I decided to do some pruning in the back yard. I was half-way through a rose bush when James came out to tell me I had a visitor at the front door. "She didn't want to come in."

Now what? I stashed my clippers and followed him into the house to find Taylor standing in the doorway.

"I know this is a bit unusual," she began, "but could you watch my dog while Megan and I go on a trip? We're going to Ireland. We'll be gone a couple of weeks."

"Taylor, I have two dogs. I don't think I can handle a third one. Could you ask someone else in the baby group?" Then I screwed up my courage and asked what had immediately popped into my mind. "Why are you going to Ireland?"

"I am so mad, Ava. Mad at myself and mad at what I let happen."

I just looked at her.

"What do I do now?" she asked. "Tim has no idea Megan and I are going to Ireland."

"Who is Tim? I asked.

"Father Timothy Damien. I just found out he has a family in Ireland."

"And does he know you are going to Ireland?"

She didn't answer.

"Taylor, I can't tell you what to do, but are you sure you want to take Megan with you? Maybe you should have your family watch her. And you should telephone Father Damien."

"He won't answer my calls."

"Have you talked to a counselor? Taylor, I don't have answers for you. If Father Damien is not answering your calls, I would worry that you might travel all that way and not be able to see him. Have you thought of that?"

Her head drooped. "Yes, I have. Oh, look at this mess I've gotten into." She took a deep breath. "I was an idiot!"

"What are you going to do, Taylor?"

"I have to talk to Tim."

"What about Brandon? Your husband?"

She shook her head. "I don't know."

"Maybe you should start with him," I said quietly.

"I feel like screaming!"

There was something she wasn't telling me, but I couldn't quite put my finger on it. "Here's what I can do for you, Taylor. I can watch Megan if you decide to get some counseling."

Her face was tight. "Okay. I'll let you know."

Later that day Mitch called to tell us Claire would be baptized. "With all the commotion going on at St. Anthony's I've decided to have it at St. Cornelius, at the other end of town."

I knew exactly what he meant.

That night, after the kids were in bed, Janel called. "From now on, Rich and I will be attending St. Cornelius."

"Taylor came over this afternoon," I volunteered. "She wants to go to Ireland."

"Funny, she came over to my house, too."

"What did she tell you?"

"She said that Father Damien is not talking to her."

"This can't end well," I said sadly.

"I think Taylor is desperate to tell everyone what happened. Maybe it's to punish Father Damien. She also said she 'has bigger problems.' I wonder what she meant by that?"

"She asked me to watch her dog," I said.

"Yeah, she asked me, too, but Rich is allergic, so I said no."

"It would be unwise for Taylor to go to Ireland if she doesn't have any contact with Father Damien."

"It would be crazy," Janel agreed.

I hung up the phone shaking my head. *Everything about the women in this baby group has been crazy. How can they sleep at night doing the things they're doing?*

That night I had trouble sleeping, thinking about Taylor and Merrick and the other women. Could I help them? I didn't agree with what they were doing, and I knew in my heart I couldn't fix their problems. So, as James would say, the thing to do was just stay out of it.

But I was finding this harder and harder since our little town was so small and everyone knew everyone else; we run into each other wherever we go.

In the morning Samantha telephoned. "My counselor thinks the baby group is a wonderful way to connect with friends who have children the same age."

I half-laughed. "Samantha, you obviously didn't tell your counselor about all the things going on with the women in the baby group."

"Oh, no," she said. "My counselor and I are talking about some of it. She thinks we're helping each other. Which reminds me, could you watch Alice while I go to the church meeting?"

"I'm sorry, Samantha, but James and I are going to that meeting, too."

"What do you think is going to happen?"

"I don't know. I honestly don't know." I was really upset about Father Damien. How could he just up and leave? James wanted to change churches, and I wondered if other people would also leave the congregation because of this.

I dropped the kids off at school and met Janel for coffee. The first thing out of her mouth was, "I hear you're not helping at the craft fair at St. Anthony's."

"That's true, I'm not. Are you?"

"No. My heart's not in it after what has happened."

"I wonder how many other people feel this way?"

She took a sip of her coffee and froze. "Ava, don't look behind you. Maria just walked in."

We didn't ask her to sit down, but the next thing I knew Maria was pulling up two chairs to join us. She touched my shoulder and I edged away and reached for Jill. I wasn't about to make small talk with an uninvited intruder, so I blurted an excuse, stood up, and moved toward the entrance.

Janel glared at me. I knew she wasn't happy to be left with Maria, but I had to get away. We had planned to go to the new park after coffee, so when Janel said, "See you," I knew exactly what she meant.

I left and drove to the park. When Janel arrived, I explained why I had left. "I want nothing to do with that woman."

Janel nodded. "When I said I had to leave, she wanted to know where I was going."

"You didn't tell her, did you?"

"Of course I didn't!"

I smiled in relief. Jill and Mandy were racing around the jungle gym and laughing; after a while they sat down for some water and I noticed two strollers rolling toward us. It turned out to be Merrick and Samantha.

In just moments we were talking about Father Damien. "I trusted him," Merrick complained. "I talked to him all the time. I hope he keeps his vow of silence about all the things I've told him."

Samantha said, "Gosh, I talked to him about personal things, too. I can't help wondering if Father Damien told Taylor anything about us."

"Wait," Janel interrupted. "He is a professional. Surely we are all wrong about this whole thing."

Samantha did not look happy. "I hope so. We should talk about this at the church meeting Tuesday night."

"I would guess it's going to get loud at that meeting," I said. "The longer people have to think about this, the angrier they will be."

"Yes," Janel agreed.

"I'm really worried about what this will do to the congregation," I said. "Part of me doesn't even want to go to the meeting."

* * *

Splashed all over the front page of the newspaper that night was a photo of Father Damien with the headline *Church in Crisis*. I scanned the article. *According to church secretary Amy Brodart, a lawsuit has been filed against Father Timothy Damien on behalf of an unnamed woman who is suing for child support for her 3-year-old daughter and an unborn child.*

An unborn child? The woman had to be Taylor, but she was pregnant?

"James, did you see this?"

"Yes. That man has made a huge mess of his life. Looks like Taylor is a disgruntled woman with a child and she's making trouble for him."

I called Janel. "Did you read the newspaper tonight?"

"Just read it."

"This is terrible. What's going to happen?"

"If we wait a day," Janel said calmly, "I bet anything Taylor will reach out to one of us."

Sure enough, the next morning, Taylor telephoned.

More Surprises

"Ava, you have to believe me when I tell you I didn't mean to have an affair with Tim."

Why should I believe her? She is sleeping with a priest who has taken a vow of celibacy. Then there's the matter of her boyfriend and her husband. I wasn't feeling too sympathetic.

"Taylor, what is going on with you?"

There was a long pause before she spoke. "My life is ruined."

"Have you seen a counselor yet?"

"I have an appointment tomorrow. What's why I'm calling. Could you watch Megan?"

"Are you going to Ireland?"

She didn't answer me for a long minute. Finally she said, "I've decided not to go. I need to talk to Tim first."

The following morning she dropped Megan off, and after the girls played in the house a while we walked to the park to meet Janel and Mandy. The girls all ran off to the jungle gym, and Janel and I settled on a bench.

"How was Taylor this morning?" Janel asked.

"Stressed out."

I had brought pails and shovels and the girls were playing in the sand, making a sand castle, when I spotted Taylor walking toward us. She looked drained.

"Well," she said, "that meeting with the counselor was something else. I am exhausted. Would you all like to come over to my house for lunch? The kids would love that."

The girls began jumping up and down, but I wondered what to say. I didn't really want to hear any more about her situation; it would just lead to finding out more upsetting things.

"That sounds great," Janel said. I shot her a look.

"The kids will love it," Taylor repeated.

I hesitated. It could only lead to more involvement in Taylor's problems, and while I wanted to know what was happening, and help her if I could, I didn't want to get too involved in her mess. Reluctantly, I agreed.

Taylor fixed the kids lunch at the kiddie table in her family room, and she and Janel and I sat in the kitchen where we could watch them. Suddenly Taylor started talking, and boy did we get an earful.

"I'm pregnant," she announced.

Janel and I stared at her.

"But I don't know whether it's Tim's or Brandon's," she added.

"Who's Tim?" Janel asked.

"Father Damien."

"What are you going to do?" Janel asked after an embarrassed silence. I couldn't think of a single thing to say.

"I don't know. I can't get hold of Tim. And I...I haven't told Brandon yet."

"*What?*" Janel and I said together.

"I've lost Tim," Taylor moaned. "I don't want to lose Brandon, too."

Or Edward, I thought. *This woman is nuts!*

"You *are* going to tell Brandon, right?" Janel said, her voice steely.

"Yes, when I find out whether the baby is his or not."

I felt sick to my stomach. How could she just sit there and talk about this like you talk about baking cookies or cleaning house?

Janel looked exasperated. "What about Edward?" I kicked her under the table and she gave a yelp.

"I am quite sure Edward is no one's father," Taylor said airily. "So I am not concerned with him any longer."

So she threw him away, just like that? I gritted my teeth to keep from saying anything.

Janel started to ask something when the doorbell rang, and Taylor went to answer it. I was extremely uncomfortable and I knew Janel could sense it. We began gathering Jill and Mandy together to leave.

When Taylor came back into the kitchen she was sniffling. "Well, I just got a special delivery letter from Tim, and—"

I cut her off. "We need to leave."

I didn't want to hear any more.

Letting the Chips Fall

A few days later I was in the kitchen pouring myself a cup of coffee when the phone rang. "I need to talk to you right away," Taylor said, her voice tense. "Can you come over this morning?"

I didn't want to be at Taylor's house. "Could we talk over the phone?"

"No, I can't talk about this over the phone. Please, Ava. Come over to my house." She sounded so desperate I couldn't refuse.

"I'll drop off the kids at school and stop by."

"Oh thank you, Ava. Thank you!" She sounded so grateful I felt guilty for hesitating.

I pulled into her driveway with an odd sense of dread and was met by Taylor at the door. "Come on in, the coffee is on." She looked pale and very tired and her voice sounded strained.

Jill and Megan ran off to the playroom; Taylor and I sat in the kitchen and she started talking.

"Tim and I have been having an affair for a long time." Her voice sounded tight. "When I became pregnant with Megan, he thought he could continue being a priest, counseling people and running the church. I knew he could not marry me; he kept saying the priesthood was his calling. Well…" She swallowed hard and continued. "Brandon and I were dating off and on, and when I told him I was pregnant, he thought it would be wonderful to have a child."

"Did you tell him the child wasn't his?"

There was a long, awkward silence, and then she shook her head. "No, I didn't. I thought Brandon was the perfect answer to my problem."

Oh, poor Brandon. Taylor has lied and played games from the beginning.

She twisted her hands together. "I can't believe I encouraged Brandon to take the promotion and move here when I knew that Tim was the father of my child. I was on a business trip when Tim and I first met. Our connection was so fast, really spontaneous…it just happened. We both regretted it, but then we couldn't resist the pull toward each other. I just wanted to be closer to him. When Brandon got this promotion I thought it was a sign. Tim told me we could never be this way again, and that's then when Edward came into my life…I guess I wasn't thinking straight."

Her voice grew shaky. "Then a few weeks ago I found out that Brandon was having an affair with Merrick. I still can't believe she would do this to me."

I couldn't believe Taylor was pointing fingers! *How can she blame Merrick for what Taylor herself was doing? This can't get any worse.*

"I'm not a bad person, Ava. Really I'm not. I need help. I don't know what to do now."

"What do you mean?" I said quickly.

"Well, the only reason I'm suing Tim is for financial support for Megan. I had no idea my personal life, and his, would be exposed in the newspaper."

"No one identifies the 'unknown woman' mentioned with you except those you yourself have told about the situation."

"But you know this little town. Sooner or later *everyone* will know." She covered her face with her hands and began to cry. "But…but that's not what I'm worried about the most."

I touched her shoulder. "Taylor, what else is wrong?"

"Brandon wants a divorce. What am I going to do now?"

"Oh, Taylor, that is really too bad. I don't know what you're going to do, but I do think you should talk to your counselor."

She heaved a shaky sigh. "My counselor says I was on a self-destructive path, and now I need to live with the consequences." Tears rolled down her cheeks.

Why does she want to tell me all this? What does she think I can do to help?

"Taylor, why are you telling *me* all this? You should be talking to your counselor."

She looked at me with reddened eyes. "I am not a bad person," she repeated. "I don't want to lose Megan. But I am pregnant again, and I honestly don't know who the father is."

She doesn't know? She is so irresponsible she doesn't know which of the three men she's been sleeping with has gotten her pregnant? I found myself growing really angry.

"I will probably lose the house and have to move someplace else, but I don't want to lose Megan. I'm afraid the court will decide I am an unfit mother."

"Why would the court be involved?"

"Brandon is going to sue for custody."

I wanted to shake her. Instead I took a moment to calm myself down. "Taylor, I guess you will have to deal with each situation as it comes along." It was all I could think of to say.

"Oh, Ava, it gets even worse."

Now what?

"Father Damien has a wife in Ireland."

"Taylor, there's no need to tell me this. Everyone knows it; the church secretary contacted the newspaper and told them everything."

"I'm telling you because I want you to know what kind of person Tim is. I want you to tell people what Father Damien did to me."

"I won't do that," I said quickly. "It's none of my business. I am not going to tell anyone anything. But I do know that you need counseling. Talk to your family; maybe they can help you."

Taylor's face suddenly looked hard. "You mean you're not going to help me out? Tell everyone what Tim did to me?"

"No. You did this to yourself, Taylor. You need to take responsibility for it, not blame Tim or Brandon or anyone but yourself." I got up from the table. "I have to leave."

"Ava, I am really disappointed in you. In fact, you bother the hell out of me! Now I know how seriously you take a true friendship, and I don't want to have anything more to do with you."

My mouth dropped open. *True friendship?* Taylor was nowhere near close to being a true friend of mine. I was speechless. Stunned, I stood there for a long minute, then I collected Jill and left.

I thought about it on the way to Janel's and I began to realize that Taylor wanted a partner in crime, so to speak. A cohort in all her drama. I didn't fall for it.

Janel was on the phone when I arrived, but she waved me into the house. I couldn't help hearing the conversation she was having. "Ava is not the problem, Taylor. *You* are the problem. You're the one having affairs with different men and having children with different fathers."

Then she was silent for a time. Finally I heard her say, "Now wait, Taylor…No, *you* listen!"

And then Janel abruptly hung up the phone and looked at me. "Taylor doesn't want to have anything to do with me anymore," she almost shouted. "Can you believe that? Like *I* did something wrong!" She was livid.

"Janel, think about it. This is Taylor's way of distancing herself from us. Everything in her world is unraveling."

That night Samantha telephoned. "I'm calling everyone about baby group this week. I just talked to Taylor, and she bit my head off."

I wasn't about to tell Samantha anything. "What are you talking about, exactly?"

"She yelled at me. She said she wished she'd never met any of us!"

"And?"

"I asked her what was wrong and she said point blank, 'I don't have time for you.'

And then she hung up on me. Can you believe that?"

"Samantha, I have no idea what has gotten into Taylor." Then I changed the subject. "Did you find a sitter so you can go to the church meeting?"

"No, not yet, but I will. I really want to know what happened with Father Damien."

"You and everyone else," I said.

To distract myself, I looked through the mail and saw a large pink envelope that contained a beautiful invitation for little Claire's christening ceremony. The date was set; all I needed to do was call Mitch and accept. I was extremely happy to focus my mind on something else.

* * *

There must have been a thousand parishioners who showed up for the church meeting. The hall wasn't big enough, so we all walked across the street to another large church that was unoccupied on a week night.

Mitch and Janel and Rich were sitting toward the front and waved James and me over. "Look at this crowd," Janel murmured.

I scooted past her. "I have a feeling this is not going to turn out well."

The new pastor, Father Flanagan, rose and began to speak. "This is a difficult time for our parish. As many of you know, there have been serious allegations regarding Father Damien, and the proper church authorities have been notified. Father Damien is cooperating fully."

"How could he do this?" a woman shouted. Then everyone started talking at once, and the new pastor had to ring a bell to get their attention.

"It should be stated that this is an isolated case." I heard sighs of disapproval around me and I looked around. An elderly woman shook her finger at Father Flanagan. He raised both hands. "I know you all want to voice your concerns, but the authorities need time to determine exactly what has occurred. However, I can tell you this. Father Damien apparently has a wife and two children who had been living in our community for some years. They are no longer here."

I looked at James. "Years?" I whispered. He shook his head.

"How long has this been going on?" a man called out.

"A wife and children? A priest can't do that!" another called.

"What about his vow of silence over all these years?" a woman shouted. "How do we know he will keep private the things we've told him in confession?"

Father Flanagan again raised his hands. "He will most certainly not reveal anything said in confidence."

An older woman shot to her feet. "How can we be sure of that?"

"Did he support his family with church funds?" someone else asked.

Father Flanagan cleared his throat. "We are looking into this. I cannot address the legal matters in this case."

The parish crowd was obviously upset. The shouting went on for a few more minutes, and then the pastor must have realized the meeting was getting out of control. "I hope you will all continue to keep your faith," he said. "God bless you all."

"That's it?" James said in an undertone. "This will drive people away from the church."

"I know," I said sadly. "This is just awful." We walked out with Janel and Rich.

"Years?" Rich said. "I wonder who his family was?"

"It's funny how you think you know a person but you don't really know them at all," I offered.

"This was a betrayal," Rich continued. "We trusted Father Damien as our priest and he threw that trust away."

"He was human," Janel said. "He made a mistake, a huge mistake. Maybe something needs to be changed in the Church? Maybe it's a sign of the times."

I wanted to believe in my church. Surely this was an isolated incident? James and I walked to our car in silence.

The following day Jill and I arrived early for gym class. The minute Janel arrived she said, "Taylor was at the meeting last night."

"What? I didn't see her. Where was she?"

"She wore a long black wig with a big hat and glasses. I had to look twice to be sure it was her."

"Did you speak to her?"

"No," she said.

"Father Damien won't take her calls. Maybe she was trying to find out where he is?"

"I don't know," Janel said, "but she looked awful in that black wig."

"Do you think she and Megan will show up for gym class today?"

"I don't know, but really, it's fine if she does. This has nothing to do with Megan's gym class."

Just then Taylor and Megan walked in. She ignored Janel and me and breezed past us without speaking. I heard her tell Megan to join the other children, and then she slowly walked to the back of the gym and sat by herself.

Samantha arrived with Alice, and then Maria, of all people, arrived with Alexis. I tensed up.

"What is she doing here?" Janel whispered.

"If she comes over, I'm going to leave and go outside. Keep an eye on Jill."

Maria sat down beside Samantha, and I heaved a sigh of relief. "Maybe Maria has moved on," I murmured.

Janel didn't answer. She was watching Taylor. "Look at her," she said. "She's all alone and she looks so sad. I feel sorry for her in a way."

"She *is* all alone," I replied. "Her life is turning upside down. It's a real mess."

The Reception

Mitch called that night and asked for the list of baby group phone numbers for the reception after Claire's christening ceremony. I hesitated. He had no idea what was going on with the women in baby group, but it wasn't my place to say anything. Before he hung up he said, "Now that I have Claire on a schedule, Brittany plans to slowly integrate her into gym class and ballet class and your baby group."

Oh, no! She should stay away from the baby group.

I called Janel. "Mitch is inviting everyone in the baby group to Claire's christening reception."

"Did you tell him everything that's going on?"

"No. It's not my place to say anything."

"Well, I'm sure he'll find out soon enough. One thing he'll discover is that you and I are avoiding the group, and he'll probably ask why."

"Then we'll have to tell him," I said.

The day of the christening my family dressed up in their Sunday best and we drove to St. Cornelius. The church was full. Samantha and Alice sat behind James and me; Janel and Rich and

Mandy were sitting with us. On the other side of the church I saw Merrick and Bobby, minus Merrick's husband, Robert.

The pastor moved the baptismal font in front of the altar, and then Mitch and Claire and Brittany walked forward. Suddenly I turned my head slightly and spied Taylor and Megan! And there was Ruthanne, too. She was wearing a beautiful short white dress, cut very low in front, with long bulky necklaces that dangled past her waist. Her jaunty hat was tilted to one side and her hair was pulled to the other side to fall in front of her body. Jane was seated next to her, but I didn't see Ruthanne's husband. I nudged Janel.

After the ceremony everyone drove over to Mitch's for the reception. He and Brittany stood at the front door, greeting the guests; they looked like a couple.

The house had changed. On my way to the bathroom I noticed all the pictures of Sonja in the long hallway had been replaced with photos of Mitch and Claire, and at the very end of the hall hung a large studio portrait of Claire, Mitch, and Brittany. I was dumbfounded. What about Sonja's memory?

But you're not here to judge; Mitch is just getting through life as best he can.

It was obvious that none of the baby group members were talking with each other. I remarked on this to Janel and then asked, "Have you seen the picture gallery in the hallway?"

She nodded. "Mitch and Brittany?"

"He must really like her," I said. "It's been less than a year since Sonja died."

Janel just smiled. "You know good men don't stay single long."

James and I and the kids stayed until cake was served, and then Mitch walked up to me. "What the heck is going on with the baby group?"

"Is it that obvious that something is wrong?"

"Yes, it is."

"Could we talk about this later? In private?"

Mitch stared at me. "Okay."

Finally all the guests left and Mitch invited me out to the porch while Claire and Jill played house. He poured a glass of wine for me and then sat down. "What's happening?"

I took a deep breath. Oh, God, this was hard to talk about. I even wondered if I *should* talk about it.

But I told Mitch everything, about Ruthanne and her drinking problem, about Merrick's having an affair with Taylor's husband, and as much about Taylor as I thought prudent. He already knew about Samantha's abusive husband.

"This is unbelievable," Mitch said.

I sipped my wine and said nothing.

"Is all the talk about Father Damien and Taylor true?"

"Yes," I said. "Brandon has asked Taylor for a divorce."

We walked silently back into the house and found the kids playing hide and seek. "Time to go home," James announced.

As we were leaving, Mitch said, "I want you both to know something. Brittany and I are seeing each other. It's serious, and I hope you will be happy for us." Brittany smiled and looked adoringly into his face.

"Good for you," I said.

James shook his hand.

Another Shock

"Janel," I said when I called her, "I told Brittany she would be welcome to bring Claire to meet with you and me and our girls, not the big baby group. She said she would like that."

"Next Wednesday?"

"Sure."

On Wednesday, Janel and Mandy and Brittany and Claire arrived at my house at the same time, and we all sat down on my quilt to watch the kids play. After that, we met every week, and then one day Janel called me and said, "Let's have baby group at my house this week."

"Sounds good."

"Bring the quilt?"

"Of course."

When Jill and I arrived at Janel's, Brittany and Claire were already there. The girls ran off to play and we sat down on my quilt. Janel brought in coffee for Brittany and me.

I was the first to spot the ring on her finger. "Brittany!"

She smiled and held her hand out. It was a beautiful diamond solitaire, and she looked ecstatic.

"This is wonderful news," I said.

Janel was quiet. I looked sideways at her and noticed how pensive she was. Wasn't she happy for Mitch and Brittany? When she and Claire left for an appointment, Janel shut the front door and came back to the quilt and sat down. She looked unusually somber.

"What's wrong?" I asked.

She drew in a long breath. "Rich has been transferred out west."

My heart dropped into my stomach. Janel was moving away from me!

"No," I said, "You can't go. You just can't. You're my best friend, and our girls are so close!"

We both started to cry. "Believe me," Janel said in a choked voice, "I told Rich I just couldn't move away. But..."

We hugged each other. "We will always be close friends," she said through her tears. "I'm just moving someplace else. I'll always have time for you, Ava."

I took her hand and we just looked at each other. "And I'll always have time for you, Janel."

And all at once I knew what I wanted to do.

* * *

James and I drove Rich and Janel and Mandy to the airport. Even Jill came. The girls giggled in the back seat; they thought a new adventure was starting and they were excited that they would get to call each other on the phone.

I already felt bereft. I sat next to Janel while the guys talked in front.

At the airport, I looked at James and he nodded and opened the back of the car to get their luggage and the package I had neatly stowed under the seat. Then we waited at the gate.

When the loudspeaker called for passengers to board their plane, I felt the color drain from my face. I hugged Janel and handed her the package. "This is for you, to remember the good times."

She opened it quickly. "Oh my God, your quilt!"

"Well, actually it's two quilts now," I said. "I made it into two twin-sized quilts, one for Mandy and one for Jill."

"Oh, Ava," she wept. "I will treasure this forever."

Then she took Mandy's hand and turned toward Rich, and they disappeared into the loading tunnel.

I don't remember the ride home.

* * *

After that the baby group fragmented. Everyone stayed to themselves, dealing with their lives and small children. Maybe too much had happened between all of us; we knew too much about each other.

When Janel left, Brittany and Claire continued to come to my house so the girls could play together, and over the years we became good friends. When Mitch and Brittany were married, only Janel and I were invited to their wedding.

Now, years later, if I run into any of the women in the baby group it's awkward. I always say hello, but there is that past history that gets in the way of the conversation. The only thing we ever talk about is the kids…everything else is off limits. Maybe some of them are embarrassed about past behavior. Or maybe when people move on they want to forget the past.

The kids started school and made new friends. No one from baby group attended Jill's school, not even in high school. James pointed out that after the baby group experience I kept most women at a distance. I guess I was hurt over the way some of the women treated me at the end.

Through the Next 25 Years

Merrick never remarried after her failed marriage. She moved away from Easthaven, and I lost touch with her.

Following years of separation, Brandon and Taylor were reunited. They raised Megan as their own, and also the new baby, Sam; Brandon was Sam's real father. I never knew what exactly happened to Father Damien. I did discover that he had been defrocked, but the church was silent on news about him or his family. The last I heard he was living in Ireland.

Brittany and I became even closer friends after Janel moved away. Mitch and Brittany were married when Claire was almost four years old, and they then had two children of their own. They remain married to this day and are very happy.

Samantha never remarried, but Greg, her ex-husband, and his boyfriend, Paul, did get married. Samantha is now thinking about moving to the city to start a new life.

Maria found the love of her life in Cheryl, who had moved to Easthaven from New York. They were married when it became legal to do so.

Ruthanne has struggled with alcoholism all her adult life and has been in and out of treatment programs. She married three times, and recently I heard she was divorcing once again. The last time I ran into her, at the supermarket, she was wearing a sheer low-cut blouse and a tight skirt with jewelry dangling from her neck and arms. She told me she was swearing off both alcohol and men.

Friendships come and go. Some are easy; some are difficult. I found a good friend in Janel, and we are still friends even though we live 2,000 miles apart. We keep in touch almost daily by telephone, and whenever James and I travel, we meet in airport terminals. Janel and Rich do the same when they fly east.

Jill and Mandy grew up and went off to college. Their quilts were well loved and quite worn, so when they left for college I took Jill's section and made a lap throw of it. Janel sent me Mandy's section and I made one up for her, too.

Jill became a doctor; Mandy ended up a physicist. They both became engaged to fine men and recently moved back to Easthaven.

Jill was Mandy's maid of honor and Mandy was Jill's when she married. Their friendship is lifelong, much like my friendship with Janel.

I had decided to do one more special thing for each of them. At Mandy's bridal shower I gave her a special gift, and I gave one to Janel as well; it was a piece of Jill's quilt, framed in a small frame for each of their homes. After I presented it, Janel dug in her large purse and pulled out gifts for Jill and me; she handed me Mandy's quilt, framed in two frames, and I cried.

Rich retired, and he and Janel eventually moved back to Easthaven. They have grandkids now, who have started their own baby groups. This last year I finished making a quilt so the infants and their moms would have a special place to gather.

Life goes on.

Afterword

I feel I am lucky to have seen my life come full circle and be able to watch in awe as my children now accept the challenge of raising their own children. I find myself looking on their lives with joy and hope for the future.

About the Author

Erina Bridget Ring was born in New York and has lived in California for 38 years. Happily married for 39 years, she has raised three children and has four grandchildren. This is her third book.

Other Books by Erina Bridget Ring

Knit 2, Purl 2, Kill 2: A Caretaker's Story of Survival
Breakfast with the FBI

56065287R00124

Made in the USA
Columbia, SC
20 April 2019